FINDING FIRE

Everything is possible.
GCLS 2017
Liz McMullen

FINDING FIRE

SHELIA POWELL & LIZ MCMULLEN

SAPPHIRE BOOKS

SALINAS, CALIFORNIA

Finding Fire
Copyright © 2017 by Shelia Powell and Liz McMullen. All rights reserved.

ISBN - 978-1-943353-71-2

This is a work of fiction - names, characters, places, and incidents are the product of the author's imagination or are used fictitiously. Any resemblance to actual persons living or dead, business, events or locales is entirely coincidental.

All rights reserved. No part of this publication may be reproduced, distributed, or transmitted in any form or by any means, including photocopying, recording, or other electronic or mechanical methods, without written permission of the publisher.

Editor - Heather Flournoy
Book Design - LJ Reynolds
Cover Design - Michelle Brodeur

Sapphire Books Publishing, LLC
P.O. Box 8142
Salinas, CA 93912
www.sapphirebooks.com

Printed in the United States of America
First Edition – February 2017

This and other Sapphire Books titles can be found at
www.sapphirebooks.com

Dedication

To every child that needs to find their way.

Acknowledgment

Shelia Powell

First of all, I have to thank Jonah B. for lending us his name and being one of our characters. You were a great inspiration!

Chris and Schileen, thanks for allowing us to continue our series. Y'all rock!

Liz, thanks for helping to bring the characters in *Finding Fire* to life. They're our babies!

And, finally, to my Sweetie I so appreciate you sharing me with people who are real to me and for loving me despite of it. Ditto.

Liz McMullen

Shelia is Southern as Southern gets and I'm an unrepentant Yankee, yet we think a lot alike. We laugh and giggle like teenagers and love spending time with the characters in our novels. I am lucky to have so much chemistry with Shelia, even though I thought she was nuts to suggest we write a series together. I've learned to trust her intuition since then, she's a psychic medium after all.

Ilia, my parents and my awesome boxer puppy Quinn are the best cheerleading squad and my most fervent supporters. Daddy cracks me up by selling lesbian paranormal novels to the conservative Christians where we live.

Thank you to Chris and Schileen for welcoming me into the Sapphire family. I appreciate your friendship and your endless dedication to every member of the Sapphire Books community: all of whom are talented and have so much to offer. Shelia and I are so fortunate that you believe in us and the Finding Home Series. Michelle Brodeur's eye-popping cover is powerful and captures Scarlett and the quest in Finding Fire. No editor is more thorough, thoughtful and methodical than Heather Flournoy. She is top notch and we are so lucky to have her. Nicki Wachner is another Sapphire sister and gifted beta reader. Her keen eye for the big picture and the smaller details helped us tighten up the story, pointed out plot holes and helped with continuity.

My best friend and copy editor Adrian Blagg came through for Shelia and I. She combed through our novel before we submitted it to Sapphire, tidying up so that the Sapphire editing team would not be bogged down by the basics, like grammar errors and typos. Thank you Adrian, I can always count on you.

Last but not least I want to thank beta readers Catherine Lane and Jaydin Nies. Catherine's fresh eyes and strong sense of story were invaluable. Finding Home is a young adult series and Shelia and I needed the teen perspective, to make sure our story, characters and dialog rang true. My grandniece Jaydin Nies did an incredible job. She's got one heck of head on her shoulders; she not only gave us the teen perspective, Jaydin also provided a comparative study of Finding Home and Finding Fire. We learned so much by seeing our series through her eyes. You're the best.

Chapter One

Molten lava swirled in her pale white irises. Scarlett Weiss's pupils were smaller than the head of a pin and as lethal as a poisonous dart. "When?" She spoke loudly to be heard over the roar of whipping wind and the growl of her Harley.

"Sinking into darkness." Maxim spoke with the dreamlike quality that accompanied his visions. "Boa is taking Magnolia to the chamber next to your father's suite."

Scarlett had to focus through a series of hairpin turns as she rode into the heart of the valley. Neither spoke. Magnolia was Scarlett's niece and the daughter of her half-sister Tia Keating. She couldn't believe that their father would kidnap his only grandchild. Something was up.

A tug in her heart drew her at a fast clip to her sister's house. Cows chewing cud in the pasture were blurs of white and black. Scarlett's rage was checked only by the desperate sorrow Tia was projecting into the woods. A tear trickled down Scarlett's cheek. It was so foreign it took her a moment to register the source of moisture. The sky was too blue to weep.

"Giovani has set the locks so only his handprint can release the mechanism."

Scarlett cursed.

"Morgana is casting a cloaking spell, but she has no idea how to temper Magnolia's light." Her niece was the most powerful firestarter that had been born in centuries. She was literally too hot to handle for most.

Maxim let out a shuddering breath. "She's terrified he will see this as a failure. Morgana's on her last chance."

The road evened out and was smoother than the country lanes. Scarlett was relieved. It was dumb luck that she hadn't wrecked the bike in her anger. "Shit."

"Has anyone ever told you that you have a way with words?" Maxim's voice was warm and spicy, like log smoke piping out of a chimney.

Scarlett chuckled. She liked her bestie's natural tenor over the creepy, I-see-dead-people voice.

"Scarlett, I'm proud of you."

She choked on her own saliva; now her eyes were nearly bulging from their sockets as she tried to expel the liquid from her lungs. "Jesus Christ, you know I'm driving."

"I know." It sounded like Maxim was smiling. "As much as I'd like to continue listening to the musical stylings of your cough, I'm wiped out."

Scarlett was still gasping, but managed to eke out, "Thanks for staying under so long. I won't forget this."

"I'll remind you of that 'round Christmas. Ta-ta for now."

The gravel path crunched loudly as she drove up the winding private drive. She looked up at the house that Tia called home. It suited her, from the wide wraparound porch with hanging baskets of flowers, to the old style Victorian vibe. The house was white, with sage colored shutters, and not a speck of flaked paint in sight. This place was well cared for, almost as well as Tia took care of the foster children that made up her family.

Scarlett worried when the estate came up on her radar. Tia was powerful, but most of her gifts were nurturing ones. Her group home was different than most foster care placements. It was a safe haven for kids with magical abilities. Scarlett kept extensive files on the people who shared her sister's home, since Tia had asked her to keep her distance. The request stung at first, but having an assassin and spy popping in on a regular basis could put the teens off balance. Erratic powers mixed with adolescent hormones was enough for one house. Scarlett respected her sister's boundaries, but hated being away when Belladonna slit poor young Angel's throat. Father must have been truly desperate to let that bitch return to the flesh.

There had been whispers on the other side. Demons were losing their caution and risking exposure—stealing powers, eating souls, and in Belladonna's case, murdering a young witch to return to the flesh. The urgency made no sense to Scarlett. Stealing his granddaughter in broad daylight was not Giovani's style. Her father was much more subtle than that. If he was desperate, the world was in trouble.

Scarlett pulled off her helmet and locked down her ride. She took in a deep breath, centering herself. She couldn't afford to be caught up in her sister's hysteria. Maxim had said the witches on this property held more strength and raw talent than any of their demonic counterparts. Scarlett balked at the idea of putting untried teenagers on the front line, but she had no choice.

Even Beau would have to join Scarlett in battle, though she had a hard time believing her half-brother was capable of anything other than comic relief and parlor room entertainment. Maxim had said Beau was more than he seemed. When she pressed for more details, he had replied, "You can't open the presents until your birthday, no peeking." *My birthday my ass.* That was Maxim's way of saying, "Neener neener, figure it out for yourself, I'm not telling."

Her black biker boots made rhythmic thuds on the paved walkway. She was just shy of the front porch when the door opened. Her sister was in a state. Tia's green eyes were wild, torn between tears of rage and despair. Her red hair was snarled from tugging. Fussing with her hair was Tia's way of dealing with stress. The mess of her waist-long curls was impressive. Magnolia couldn't have been gone more than an hour.

Scarlett took the stairs two at a time and drew Tia into her arms. She may have been a good fifteen years younger than Tia, but she was the protector, even when they were kids. "I'm sorry I couldn't get here in time."

Tia pulled back from her embrace. "You knew the bastards were going to take my baby?"

"No," Scarlett barked, then softened her tone. "I may not be a regular part of Magnolia's life, but my niece is precious to me." Having to stay away hurt more than Scarlett was willing to admit. "I would never let Father get his evil little hands on her. He's crossed the line this time, and that means war." Scarlett wasn't being dramatic. She meant exactly what she said. Kidnapping Magnolia was an act of war.

Scarlett followed her sister into the house. Tia's silence was more disturbing than her earlier outburst. That scared Scarlett; her sister was normally unflappable. Then again, she knew the monster who took her daughter. His involvement would rattle the most battle-hardened soldier.

Two teenagers trampled down the stairs like a herd of elephants. "Not exactly known for stealth," Scarlett teased, her smile sardonic.

"Who the fuck are you?" the blue-haired punk rock girl asked with a shudder-worthy growl. She had been dropped on Tia's doorstep, but not as a baby in a basket. Her parents were terrified of her abilities. Shorting out the electricity in her parents' mansion had been the last straw. They were lucky the blue sparks hadn't set the house on fire.

Scarlett liked her instantly and her smile even reached her eyes when she introduced herself. "The name's Scarlett. I'm Tia's half-sister." Scarlett was only a couple of years older than the teen, but in the Dark Realm an eighteen-year-old was considered a full-on adult. There was no coasting through college and finding yourself. A demon's childhood ended the moment their powers quickened.

"Pasty bitch." Her laugh was cruel and biting, just like her words. "Shit, you're completely colorless." Her uncensored distaste made Scarlett like her even more.

"Finally, you have someone interesting in this house." Scarlett turned to her sister and said, "What do ya call her, 'Switchblade'?"

"She's Lilith, and I'm Kayla." Kayla's smile was wan. The teenager seemed a watermark of the usual self Tia had described. Pain and loss had changed Kayla. Scarlett knew the teen was trying and that was a good start. She needed her strong for the upcoming battle. "Pleased to meet you." She offered her hand first to Kayla, which made Lilith snarl. *Ah, more than friends, interesting.*

Lilith's handshake was a work of art, iron strong

with just enough electricity to give off blue sparks. "Sure I can't call you Livewire? That's a neat trick."

Lilith's eyes narrowed and electric blue flame swirled in her eyes.

"Have you ever mixed your blue fire with red?" Scarlett asked conversationally.

Lilith raised a finely sculpted, dark blue eyebrow.

"We could melt the Empire State Building with some practice."

"You're not kidding," Lilith said, the slight relaxation in her pose betraying her interest.

"Not at all. If we bring Kayla into the mix, we can blast a hole clean through my father's fortress."

"Rad." This time the blue sparks sang with excitement, witch wind fluttering Lilith's blue pigtails.

"Oh look, trouble's come to town," an elegant older woman teased as she joined the group.

"You have no idea," Scarlett quipped. She loved Sophia, and wished she had been her mom. Maybe she would have turned out normal and nice—like Tia. Scarlett repressed the sigh that had built up. Nothing could change the damnation of her birth. She looked forward to using her darker magic against her father. They would get little Magnolia back, and this time, her father would pay with his soul. Scarlett smiled. A few good friends would fight over the right to swallow his evil soul and damn it to the depths of hell. *A girl can dream.*

Chapter Two

"Let's go check in on the tragic prince, shall we?" Scarlett asked as she walked through the kitchen and took the back stairs to the second floor. Tia harrumphed then followed. Luke Matthews had nearly drowned thanks to the demons targeting Tia's foster children. Scarlett opened the bedroom door and repressed a gasp. Luke looked like a fallen angel. His skin was pale, with the exception of the livid bruises in the shape of thick chain links around his neck. She almost abandoned her plan, but she couldn't let her heart make decisions. It was incredibly unreliable and she had a soft spot for brooding boys with brown eyes.

Scarlett knew she was about to blow Luke's cover, but it was necessary. He needed to believe she was omniscient, that Scarlett knew all of his secrets, that way he would never be tempted to lie to her.

"Luke, I'm Tia's half-sister, and I'm here to help. You have the chance to play a pivotal role in our plan to rescue Magnolia, but first I need you to be honest with me, and I need you to tell Tia the truth."

Luke's muscular body grew as hard as carved granite. She let Luke swing in the wind a bit. Scarlett could see the storm clouds in his eyes as he tried to nail down the lie she was about to expose. Her sister was less willing to keep her silence. This was one of her kids, after all.

"Scarlett, Luke has many faults, but I've never

caught him in a lie. And you know I would be able to tell." Tia could read minds like nobody's business. Scarlett could sense Tia mentally pacing the floor in agitation.

"It was a lie that was born before he met you, but one he is desperate to keep." She looked deep into his brown eyes, waiting for the moment he saw what she was after. He started to shake.

Tia was quickly at his side, pulled the blanket from the foot of the bed and tucked it around him. "What have you done?"

"Nothing. No spells cast," she promised, giving Tia a three-finger salute. "Scout's honor. Besides, you would feel my magic if I tried to harm a hair on his pretty little head."

Luke slipped from Tia's grasp, and bless his heart, stood toe-to-toe with Scarlett. She didn't move or react physically in any way. She knew what she had to do to make him recoil, and it wasn't her strong right hook. "You're not a child now, are you?"

Luke grew pale, and as expected, backed away from Scarlett. Tia looked dumbfounded. There was no masking that level of shock.

"You haven't been for quite some time." Scarlett leaned against the doorframe, her motorcycle boots crossed at the ankle.

"What the hell are you talkin' about? He may age out of the system next month, but he's still a minor." Tia's conviction was solid, but her distress was obvious in the tense lines around her mouth.

"First of all, his birthday is not next month, it's July eighth. I thought you could spot a Cancer sign from a mile away. Especially one who is an extreme empath." Scarlett ticked off one finger, then launched into her next bombshell. "Not only isn't he a minor, he wasn't one when you took him in."

Tia froze. She didn't have one southern fried comment.

Luke was trembling full force, his biggest fear and deepest secret exposed. Scarlett was worried he might take a spill and hurt himself. "Luke, please take a seat, I don't want you to fall. I'm not your enemy. I simply don't want to start our friendship with lies and you need to fess up to Tia. Don't underestimate her compassion. She wouldn't kick you out of her home, regardless of your birth date. You're an empath...you know she doesn't have it in her to hurt you. She loves you."

Luke, with Tia's support, sat down on the bed. Tears were streaming down his face. Scarlett may have been a bitch, but she wasn't heartless. She knew he was too upset to share his truth. "Tia, Luke's turning twenty-one this summer. He's wanted to tell you all along, hated lying to you, but he couldn't risk being sent away."

Tia pulled him into her arms. "Is that true honey?"

Luke nodded. "I just, I've never felt at home anywhere." His expression was pained. He didn't even try to brush away his tears. "I never belonged. Even now I don't exactly fit in."

"Your name isn't Luke, either. Tell Tia what happened."

It took a while for Luke to gather himself, but when he did, he came clean completely. "My name is Tanner Mathews, and I'm from New Jersey." He sucked in a breath as he gathered his courage. "Our house was demolished during Superstorm Sandy, my parents died and my…"

Scarlett sat down and flanked Luke, so both sisters could offer him comfort. She knew he was a liar, but she didn't know the truth behind the lie.

"My little brother Luke died. I had just turned seventeen and I lost my entire family." Scarlett felt the glow as Tia sent Luke healing energy. "Our house was gone. Everything was so pulpy and mashed up, the only thing I had was my brother's sopping wet social security card and birth certificate, and a backpack's worth of clothes." Luke ran his hands through his short brown hair, then covered his face. "God I can't believe it's been four years. I ache like the last day I saw my neighborhood." He pressed his hand to his chest as if he could stem the flow of pain flooding his system.

"Go on, honey. I know you're almost done," Tia encouraged.

"I hitchhiked up here. I thought I could live on the streets, but my powers had exploded during the storm. I felt more than I could handle, even ended up in a nuthouse, under my brother's name." Luke held his arms tight to his body. "When I was deemed healthy enough for society, I was thrown into the foster care system. They thought my breakdown came from grief." A tear slipped from his thick lashes, then landed on his sleep pants. "The grief was there, but…I didn't have a name for what else I was feeling and I was too afraid to strike out on my own."

Luke sat up straighter, moving away from their embrace. As if coordinated, both sisters stood and gave Luke some room to breathe. The young man was too raw to be comforted, and his empathic abilities made it impossible for him to be touched physically. Their emotions were clearly clouding his. "Winter Casey, my social worker, got me when I was too beaten down to cope and put me here with Tia." He ruffled his hair hard, scratching his scalp in frustration. "For the first time since I lost my family, I felt safe. I couldn't give that up. I couldn't let Tia know how old I really was."

"Oh sweetie, even if you were ninety years old I wouldn't show you the door." She smiled at Luke but didn't draw closer. "You're my family, and that's that. Now can I hug you or what?"

Luke nodded and Tia folded him into her arms. Scarlett kept her distance as the two finally shared a connection not tangled by lies.

"I have a bit of good news for you, Luke. It was your deception that was holding back your abilities. You sucked at summoning animals because you couldn't forgive yourself for lying." Scarlett smirked when fire lit up his eyes, just garden-variety outrage and indignation since Luke wasn't a fire witch.

Scarlett walked to the window that faced the roadway, taking in the little piece of heaven Tia had carved out for her family. Rolling hills of green surrounded a covered bridge that spanned over a modest waterfall. The babbling brook glistened in the sunlight as its gentle current passed over smooth rocks and lush vegetation. She felt a pang in her heart, a brief one, but a true ache for a normal life and a loving home. She was grown now, and there was no going back. She was less likely than Lilith to fit in with Glinda and her good witches.

She tapped the cool windowpane with a blunt fingernail. "You were protecting your secret with a white-knuckle grip. There wasn't room for you to do anything other than tread water." She grimaced, remembering his capture and near-drowning only weeks before. "More than that, you couldn't forgive yourself for living. Survivor's guilt." She reached up to caress Luke's cheek. She felt for him and all he'd lived through. "I can help you hone your skills."

Tia was visibly startled by her offer, but hid it with some humor. "You, the All Powerful Scarlett Weiss, are going to train somebody?"

"You know I'm not quite that altruistic. We need his help and Luke has to be all in, without lies or fear clouding his abilities."

Tia wrapped Scarlett up in a big hug. She whispered into her ear, "Thank you, you big ol' softie."

Scarlett leaned back to look into her sister's lovely green eyes. "I learned from the best."

Chapter Three

"Luke, let's see about this." Scarlett hovered her right hand above the angry bruises on his neck. They should have been gone by now, especially with the combined efforts of the healers in the house, but the wounds lingered painfully. Sophia and her apprentice Terrance had tried their best. Terrance had even called up Memaw from New Orleans. His grandmother's healing abilities were legendary. The effort took a lot out of Memaw, so Terrance returned with her to Louisiana to help her regain her strength. Scarlett had some suspicions as to why their healing magic was unsuccessful, but she would need to examine him to confirm her intuition.

"Luke, you don't have to worry about me reading your thoughts; that's my sister's bailiwick." Her ponytail was too tight, so she removed the elastic band. Her waist-long white hair was heavy and she didn't like wisps tickling her face when she was spell casting. Once her hair was up in a bun, she continued. "I can, however, see the signatures of magic. Even with Memaw pitching in, these wounds would never heal."

Tia gasped in shock.

Luke turned a ghastly shade of grey. "Never?" he croaked, his throat too injured for normal speech. He touched his neck unconsciously and cringed. The dark bruises were incredibly tender.

"Not without the counterspell. To break a spell

this tightly bound, you need to know the demon who cast it." Scarlett sat beside Luke and patted his hand. "I've been known to break my father's spells from time to time. So don't give up hope just yet."

Cold blue tendrils hovered above the injury, invisible to the naked eye, but she was no ordinary witch. Scarlett reached out, her fingers glowing as they encountered the curse. She gritted her teeth in anger. Someone of her blood did do this, but not her father. She closed her eyes and probed deeper past the cloaking spell to the heart of the demon who tried to drown two of Tia's foster children.

A pang of sadness hit her heart when the demon's identity was revealed. "Rayne." It was her brother. Rayne had been seeking their father's approval for his entire life. It was unattainable for him, yet still he tried.

Tia's expression hardened. "Both times?"

"I'd have to examine Kayla, but there is no doubt who did this." Scarlett gestured to Luke's injuries then thought about the girls downstairs. Kayla's girlfriend wouldn't like Scarlett getting close enough to examine Kayla, but Scarlett didn't have time to accommodate Lilith's ego and temper.

"The bigger question is why?" Scarlett was mystified. What could Rayne possibly get out of this?

"He tried to kill both of my babies and stole my little girl."

"Kayla and Luke, yes. Magnolia, unlikely. Maxim's vision involved Father. He would never include Rayne in something this important." Scarlett got up and walked around the room as she thought things through. She would need to do some digging first. This mystery was too tangled for easy interpretation.

"I'm going to wring his neck," Tia said with

venom, which made Luke flinch. "Oh sweetie, I'm sorry. That was an unfortunate choice of words." She sat beside him on the bed, and gave his hand a reassuring touch.

"Usually his motivations are clear. Rayne is not known for his subtlety. But this is something else. I'm going to need to do some research. I'd like to walk the scene without any preconceived notions, then interview everyone in the house."

There was a soft knock on the door, "Can I come in?"

"Of course, Beau. Join the party," Scarlett invited.

"I've been listening in, and wanted to offer myself as a guide for your investigation. I can take you places without explaining their significance. Plus, I think it's best to keep the kids, Sophia, and Tia here while we are out."

"So you used the glass against the doorway trick?"

Beau laughed, but his smile didn't reach his eyes. "No, I heard you from downstairs." He raised his hand to forestall their alarmed reactions, then said, "Magnolia's absence has flipped a switch in my head. I'm listening to everything, whether I like it or not. I'd prefer to put the volume down on Kayla and Lilith, though. Their courting is making things awkward."

Scarlett laughed. "I'll teach you how to compartmentalize. For now I think this will help." She rested her hand on her brother's brow, breaking the connections to messages he did not need to hear. "Think of it a parental block on certain TV channels."

Beau's shoulders sagged with relief. "Thank God. Those two were driving me nuts."

Scarlett joined Beau at the threshold of the closed door. "Beau, I'm going to need some of your clair action."

"Claire action?" Luke croaked. "Beau has a girlfriend?" He was dead serious and so was the situation; no one laughed at him.

Tia, ever the teacher, clued her kid in. "Claircognizant, clairvoyant, clairaudient, clairsentient, and clairgustant. Don't you cross your eyes at me young man." Her smile was grim. "Clear sight is just a lot of different ways of knowing things: either how things are or how they will be. The information can come from thought, sight, sound, emotion, and taste. Beau can—"

Scarlett heard wood creaking. A strong wind buffeted the windows, rattling them. The house and grounds were as unsettled as her sister. "As much as I appreciate the magical primer, there are more pressing matters."

Tia looked like she was going to sass back, like when they were kids, but she held her tongue. This was about her baby, and she clearly was relying on Scarlett to make things right. That responsibility of trust weighed heavily; Scarlett was not used to people counting on her.

Beau was usually the one to soften things up with a joke, but her favorite ginger-haired brother was pissed off. Scarlett kinda liked the rise of color in his cheeks. "Beau, I know Rayne has been at the center of things here, but I can't for the life of me understand why he would think killing Tia's kids would make Daddy proud."

Luke swayed. Unchecked, the effects of the spell would continue to sap his energy until he passed away. She didn't need him to make more work for her by injuring himself further. "Luke, can you lie back down?"

He complied, but she could tell Luke's patience was wearing thin. His lips pressed together as if he was trying to hold back a string of cuss words that would make Scarlett proud.

Beau gestured to the head of the bed. "Scarlett, come on over and hold my hand, but no funny business." He had a slight glimmer in his eyes. Humor was never far away from Beau, and Scarlett loved him for it. She held his hand without comment.

He guided them until they were standing beside the pillow. "I'll hover above his brow with my left hand, and you do the same above his Adam's apple with your right hand." Once the connection was made, a sigh of witch wind ruffled the fine hair beside her cheeks and chilled her skin as their powers rose.

A vision of that night formed, one only Beau and Scarlett could see. A loud thumping and an icy mist met each wooden blade as the waterwheel smacked the river, slowly dragging Luke's chained form under the surface. The chain links that bound Luke's neck and ankles were thick enough to rip down an oak tree. Scarlett shivered. Beau squeezed her hand to keep her grounded in the here and now.

Beau reached into the past with his index finger and thumb pressed together, then slowly opened his fingers as if he was zooming in to take a picture with his cell phone. Scarlett lurched forward as they were drawn into the vision. They dangled twelve feet above the roiling spray.

Softly at first, then with more punch, Scarlett heard Rayne chanting. Each time he repeated the ancient words, the chain around Luke's neck tightened. Scarlett reached out; she couldn't let Rayne crush Luke's throat.

"You can't help him honey. Now stop squirmin'. I'm trying to figure out what this knucklehead was thinking." Beau shuddered. Scarlett knew he didn't like playing hide-and-seek games in people's heads. He never had, even with Sophia and Tia there to keep him grounded in this world.

Unfortunately, Scarlett was along for the ride. Soon they entered Rayne's twisted head, and could hear his thoughts.

Not so brave now, pretty boy. Father was right. Vermin and rejects, that's all you are. Tia loves broken dolls, and I'm going to rip the island of misfit toys apart. One pathetic life after the other.

Rayne could sense Belladonna behind him. *Once you are back in the flesh, I'm going to take you, too. Xavier has no true power. I'll squash him like a roach under my boot.*

There was a knock on the door, breaking the connection to the past with a painful snap. Luke's face was ashen. Tia brushed Beau and Scarlett aside so she could send healing light into the boy's shivering form. Luke may not have been privy to their vision, but he obviously could feel the icy chill seeping from their hands.

Scarlett willed out the cold as she opened and closed her fists. She didn't risk fire. A rapid change in temperature could damage the finer workings of her hands.

"It's Kayla. Let me in." Not bothering to wait for a response, Kayla crashed into the room, flames licking at her fingertips. Her eyes darted around, looking for the enemy. "What the fuck is going on?"

Beau was at her side, soothing her with white light. Kayla's flames flickered then dissipated in a puff of smoke.

Lilith yelled from downstairs, "If you don't let me the fuck out of here, I'm going to torch the entire house." Lilith's anger made the house tremble. The air smelled like an electrical storm was brewing.

"Kayla, what did you do to poor Lilith?" Beau asked, laughter dancing in his green eyes.

Kayla thundered down the stairs and yelled back, "I just told her to stay put."

Everyone from the bedroom ran after her; even Luke shuffled down the stairs. Scarlett covered her mouth and tried to repress the giggles. Beau's slack-jawed amazement was not helping matters.

Lilith was shouting obscenities and dark promises. The doorway to the meditation room was blocked with a force field that looked like a soap bubble, but it crackled with menace each time Lilith tried to break through.

Kayla's mouth was opening and closing, but she remained speechless.

Sophia jogged into the hallway. "Kayla, you set this force field. If Scarlett tries to break it, she might hurt Lilith."

"Don't you dare!" Lilith looked like she was going to tear the walls from their studs. "Kayla, you did this, fix it."

Tia rested her hands on Kayla's shoulders, lending her quiet support.

"I don't know how," Kayla said as she gestured toward Lilith. The force field pushed free from the threshold, then encircled Lilith in a shimmering bubble.

Lilith was trying to blast out of it, but the electricity just rimmed the surface like a giant plasma globe from a science exhibit. She growled and tried harder.

"Outta my way," Beau said as he pushed past Kayla and Scarlett. He raised his hands and started chanting. Witch wind swirled about the room, making the bubble tremble. He pointed both hands at Lilith. A powerful gust of wind broke the bubble and Lilith landed on her ass.

Lilith's mouth dropped open. She stared at Beau as if he had grown a few extra heads and a horn. Scarlett couldn't blame her; it was easy to forget how powerful Beau was. He was usually a one-man theater troupe, making everyone laugh. "Put your tongue back in your mouth, Bluebell. Beau is a very powerful being. He just chooses to hide it behind his crazy antics."

Scarlett winked at her brother, then used magic to help Lilith back on her feet. Lilith opened her mouth to say something very special, no doubt, but was interrupted by Sophia's calm hospitality. "Who wants a tall glass of sweet tea?"

Chapter Four

"Oh my God, I can hardly stand it!" Maxim nearly squealed with delight.

Scarlett's bestie stood in the doorway to the kitchen. He was a glamorous nugget of a man whose posh style and boyish good looks had seduced many demons, male and female. "What brings you to this side of the world? I thought you'd rather eat glass than be with us commoners." She wanted to pick him up and swing him around, mostly because he would absolutely hate it. She was finding it hard to resist.

Maxim put up his hand. "Don't you dare. Just because I am portable, doesn't mean you can play with me like a dolly. Besides, that's not exactly your toy of—"

Scarlett cut him off before he got too personal. "Okay, now that we have that straightened out." Maxim snickered at the word straight, he couldn't help himself. "Why didn't you just watch from your *throne room*?"

"This is must-see-TV, no way I was going to record it. I wanted to see Lilith go all electric snow globe, up close and personal."

"Who invited the mini Ken doll?" Lilith was seething.

It was a fair characterization. Maxim was blond, blue-eyed, and had a perfect smile, which was more like a smirk at the moment. Scarlett was tempted to join in the act, but she restrained herself, barely.

Scarlett had her eye on Lilith and prepared for a burst of electricity, her hands ready to deflect it from her bestie. Maxim was a powerful seer but he couldn't block for shit. "Play nice, Maxim, or I'll toss you back into your realm." Scarlett called up a shimmering portal, the surface like liquid silver.

"Primitive but serviceable." Maxim was a magic snob. Portals and scrying were his specialty.

Scarlett gave him an *oh really* look.

"Fine, fine, I'll be civil, just keep Blueberry Muffin away from me."

A swift wave of Scarlett's hand made the portal fade to smoke, and removed the temptation of giving Maxim a swift kick into oblivion. Lilith's twitching trigger finger was giving off sparks. Scarlett was caught between letting Lilith make a move and not torching her sister's house.

Lilith growled, her irises a swirl of electric blue anger. "I've fucking had enough of this shit. Someone's got Magnolia and I don't trust Milkshake and Small Fry. They might be the ones behind the kidnapping."

Ice cubes clinked loudly as Sophia tugged the pitcher of iced tea out of the fridge. The sound distracted Lilith enough for Scarlett to get in a better defensive position. Teenagers with powers were unpredictable, and at times, deadly.

"Sophia, I take your Southern hospitality and raise you this." Maxim waved his hand and the long dinner table was populated with tall glasses of sweet tea at each setting, along with fruit, pastries, and other niceties. "Sorry Lilith." Maxim's apology was half-assed. The electric glimmer in Lilith's eyes showed that she knew it. "I should stop trying to flip your switches."

The teenager balled up her fists. The scent of ozone filled the room, a warning sign for the impending thunderstorm. Scarlett widened her stance, and Maxim gave the teenager a look that said, *bring it*.

A loud growling stomach broke the tension. All eyes turned to Kayla. The teenager's pale white skin flushed. She looked like she'd rather be anywhere but the focus of attention.

Lilith laughed and the sparks floating around her hands winked out. "Oh my God. Are you toting an alien in there?"

Kayla hid behind her chin-length black bangs. "What? I haven't eaten much for days."

Lilith's snarky expression smoothed into tender concern. She gently took Kayla's hand in hers, offering support. "Glad to have you back."

Scarlett felt for Kayla. Her mind must have been spinning with the rapid turn of events. She was forced to watch her best friend's murder and was catatonic with grief for weeks. Kayla was slowly killing herself by not eating. The kiss she shared with Lilith had snapped her out of it, but was abruptly interrupted by a frantic Tia. The door to Kayla's bedroom had swung so wide and fast that the doorknob dented the drywall. Kayla must have been thunderstruck by the news that Magnolia had been kidnapped. It was her worst nightmare come to life.

Lilith squeezed Kayla's hand as they shared an intimate moment. The rest of the folks in the room busied themselves and took a seat at the table to give the teens some privacy. Scarlett snagged a cheese pastry and practically inhaled its sweet, flaky goodness.

"You a bit hungry, sis?" Tia's Southern accent was playful.

Three strawberries later, Scarlett said, "A tad. I'm eating on Kayla's behalf."

Sophia fixed two plates filled with fruit and muffins, and walked toward the teens. "You go on and eat this upstairs."

Lilith reached for one of the plates.

"These are for Kayla. You oughta fix yourself somethin'."

To Scarlett's surprise, Lilith obeyed immediately, but Sophia stopped her before she got far. "I was kiddin'. Text Tia if you need more provisions."

Kayla called out a thank you over the banister and was soon out of sight.

"Now that they're taken care of, let's get down to it," Tia said as she ran her fingers through her tousled red curls. "I want my baby back. You got a plan?"

"As a matter of fact I do." Scarlett rolled up her cuffs revealing her gauntlet tattoos on both forearms. The black tribal design had a flame motif that stood out starkly from her white albino skin. She tilted her head to the side until it made a cracking sound.

"I hate when you do that." Tia shuddered.

Scarlett smirked. "That's why I did it Ti-tia. First thing we need to do is check in on Magnolia, make sure she's okay."

"What do you mean check? If we can check, why not just bring her home?" Tia's chair scraped as she stood. Her pacing was making Scarlett dizzy, so she decided to focus on Sophia instead. Just looking at the woman was soothing.

Beau spoke up. "Sis, she means we need to enchant a mirror, a witchy version of a baby monitor." Scarlett was taken aback by Beau's deeply serious tone. He looked calm, but Scarlett could feel his magic and it was more distracting than Tia wearing a hole in the wooden floors. "If Father has her, she is going to be locked down tight. Good thing my niece is too bright to cloak completely. That way we can look in on her."

Tia didn't look convinced. "I can't just leave her with him. You know what happens if you spend too much time on the other side. It will darken her without spells." Beau stood up and opened his arms. Tia fell into the hug and allowed herself to cry. Her soft sobs were breaking Scarlett's heart.

"Now for that, I actually do have a plan." Scarlett always felt better when she could be useful. Sitting around and doing nothing was not her thing. "At first I was going to fix a potion to break the aging spell, but it wouldn't be too hard to add some protection against darkness."

Tia was angry. She didn't bother wiping away her tears. "Why the fuck didn't you break the spell in the first place? Do you know what it did to me to watch my baby girl turn into a tween before her time?"

"Tia, language," Sophia said.

Tia balked at being corrected, but held her tongue.

When Magnolia was born, her soul was very mature. She was wise beyond her years, but the expression of that wisdom and working magic came with a price. Each time her old soul came to the surface, Magnolia aged physically. When *The Darkness* tried to kill Kayla and Luke, she aged a few years. Angel's murder clicked the fast forward button, turning Magnolia from a toddler into a ten-year-old.

"It takes strong magic to break the curse. That kind of magic costs the spell caster dearly." Scarlett put her arm around her sister's shoulders, forging a connection. "She was not in danger until now."

"You don't think he would hurt her, would he?" Tia tugged on her hair, and Scarlett rested her hand on her sister's, urging her to let it go.

Scarlett pursed her lips as she tried to find words that would soften the truth. "Not in the way you think. He wouldn't physically harm her, but he might try to charm Magnolia into using magic for dark things. It would start mild, like opening the lid on the cookie jar and stealing a cookie. The next time he would up the ante and slowly draw her into using darker magic."

"I will crack his skull and shove his brains down his throat if he harms one hair on Magnolia's head." Bloodthirsty Beau was alarming. He would need to dial it down a notch if they were going take Magnolia back.

"Maxim, you get Beau started on that mirror. I'll catch up with you in a minute." Both men took the back stairs to the attic to hunt down the right mirror and enchant it.

"Tia, you should walk the property with me," Scarlett said. "I need to get further inside Rayne's pitiful head and see what his endgame is. After that, we need to go where Luke was tortured."

A pained gasp came from the end of the table. Scarlett had completely forgotten Luke was in room. "Sorry, sometimes I can be blunt."

"Ya think?" Tia said.

"Once I've gotten all I can get from the crime scenes, I need to go to other side and start gathering the ingredients for the potion. Some things only grow in darker places."

Sophia rested her hand on Scarlett's shoulder. Her white hair was like a halo about her head, and the concern in her green eyes was real. It made Scarlett's heart beat faster. She didn't get to spend much time with people who cared about her. In her line of work, loyalties were like shifting sands. Everything was negotiable when the price was right.

"I'm worried about you headin' out alone like this. Your father can be unpredictable. Something tells me that he's going to be on edge." Sophia sat heavily in the chair across from Scarlett. "I regret the day I met the man."

Tia's face fell. It took Scarlett a moment to figure out why that made her sister so sad. Then it came to her. If Giovani and Sophia hadn't met, Tia and Beau wouldn't have been born.

Sophia looked stricken; her aura radiated pain. "Not in that way. You both have always been a blessing in my life. Your light and love gave me the courage to leave him." Her hand trembled on the table's worn wooden surface. "I still can't believe he let me go."

"At least my mother was good for something other than cracking skulls and eating souls." Scarlett's birth mother was a succubus and an unrepentant assassin. She was younger and used her ripe body to steal Giovani's affections. "Vivian. Just saying her name leaves a sour taste in my mouth. Shame I took up the family business."

Tia looked like she was about to comment, but Sophia stopped her with a light press of her hand on Tia's forearm. Scarlett appreciated the considerate move. Tia always had a lot to say about how Scarlett made a living.

Sophia's kindness both healed and hurt Scarlett. Scarlett willed the ache from her heart. She loved this place, but it left her shields wide open. Worst of all, it made her feel emotions that could make her hesitate or put lives at risk. "Hate to cut this heart-to-heart short, but we're losing light. Maxim is going to need my help to scry for Magnolia, then we need to get a move on." She paused. Maybe examining the hauntings in darkness would give her more insight. All but Kayla's cliff dive occurred after sunset.

Scarlett assessed each person in the room, measuring their abilities and usefulness. "Maybe we need to slow down. Emotion and urgency can lead to careless work. This is far too important. Sophia, you should come upstairs. We need a witness and you are so good at reading situations. For once not having powers will work in your favor."

"How do ya figure that?" Tia asked, her body practically vibrating with the desire to act. Scarlett would have to keep her sister on a tight leash since she couldn't trust her to stay out of things. Normally Scarlett would set Beau on watch, but his rage had rendered him even more vulnerable to rash decisions.

"We see things that are invisible to the naked eye. The problem is, we won't know if what we are seeing is real or whether the vision is past or premonition." What she wanted to say was Tia was too close to this to be objective and reliable. Losing her baby girl obliterated her common sense. "Without second sight, Sophia will be anchored in the here and now, and may pick up on things we would miss because of our abilities."

Sophia brightened. She wasn't much different than Scarlett—they were both doers. "I'll help in the best way I can, but I will need to stand behind your shields. I can't block scrying or avoid leaving psychic footprints when I focus too hard."

"Between Maxim and me, we got you covered," Scarlett confirmed.

Sophia gestured toward the other side of the kitchen. "You two go on upstairs. I need to find my reading glasses first."

Tia pointed at the object in question, which was hanging around her mother's neck from a silver chain. "They're right there, Mama."

"Oh." Sophia's ivory skin colored slightly. "So they are. I'm allowed a senior moment or two."

Tia stood and offered her mother a hand up, even though Sophia was more than capable of rising on her own. The yoga positions she managed during meditation would make a contortionist envious.

"Come on over, Scarlett. Let's hug it out," Tia said as she opened her arms in welcome to both.

Scarlett paused. She was going to beg off but decided not to be a pain in the ass. The hug felt good, filled with Tia's light magic and Sophia's unconditional love. Scarlett soaked up the healing energy. She doubted there'd be time to rest once this train left the station.

"Come on, we need to play mirror, mirror on the wall," Tia said as she stepped out of the hug.

Sophia smiled. "We can't let the boys have all the fun. Besides, we need to be sure Lilith doesn't sneak up on Maxim and give him a taste of one of her lightning bolts."

That thought propelled Scarlett up the stairs, two risers at a time. It wasn't just Lilith she was worried about. Kayla could make some drama on her own, especially since she had absolutely no control of her latest ability. Scarlett was pretty sure that creating magic traps and cages was only the surface of what she was capable of. Scarlett didn't want to have to track Maxim if Kayla accidentally opened a portal. Without supervision, Lilith could seize on the possibility and punt Maxim into another realm.

    The sound of shouting made Scarlett pick up her pace. She was halfway into the attic when she saw Maxim floating five feet above the ground. Kayla looked up in horror. Scarlett sighed. The damn kid was going to be trouble.

    Lilith was bouncing a ball of electricity on her open palm. "My, my, Ken Doll. You're looking tall now." Her chuckle was throaty and cruel. "Wanna dance?"

Chapter Five

With a wave of Scarlett's hand, Lilith's electric ball shorted out. She surrounded Lilith with a glowing red force field. The terror in the teen's eyes assured Scarlett that she wouldn't be throwing any lightning bolts.

Scarlett reached up in Maxim's direction and made a wrenching motion with her hand. Kayla's accidental magic snapped away. Gravity was going to give her good friend quite a wallop. She gestured with both hands, stopping his free fall and sending him at high speed into her open arms.

Maxim, cheeky in the face of danger, quipped, "My hero. Shall we kiss?"

Scarlett set her bestie on his feet. "I didn't think I was your type. I'm missing the required equipment."

He harrumphed. "You're butchier than Luke, our tragic prince." Maxim fanned himself. "That one gives me the vapors."

Luke was the last person to enter the room. Unfortunately, he was there in time to hear Maxim's backhanded compliment. His pale cheeks took on a charming rosy hue. Thankfully, he was speechless.

"Be that as it may." She looked down at her saucy best friend and guessed this wasn't an unprovoked event. "What did you say?"

"When Punky Smurf entered the room, she wasn't particularly ladylike."

Lilith was sweating, the heat from the cage causing her makeup to run. She looked like she wanted to flash fry all of them. As much as Scarlett would like to melt the vivid blue pigtails on the mouthy teen, she needed Tia on her side.

"Tia, be sure to walk up close to her before I remove the cage. She's likely to turn Maxim and me into chicken fried steak if I remove it at this distance."

Scarlett released Lilith. When the teen looked ready to lunge, Tia grabbed hold of her hand. "Lilith, I expected more from you."

The wicked smile on Lilith's face winked out.

Tia looked the teen right in the eyes, and the swirl of anger in her irises stilled to a startling blue. "Did you send Maxim into the rafters?"

Kayla put her body between Tia and Lilith. "That was me again. Lilith didn't do anything." The protective display was another sign that Kayla was clawing out of the haze that followed Angel's murder.

"I have no idea what's going on," Kayla said. Her stance was both defensive and vulnerable. "This is worse than setting the house on fire."

Thanks to Maxim, Scarlett had complete dossiers on each of the foster kids that Tia took on. Kayla had been quite the accidental pyromaniac when her powers first quickened as a tween. Scarlett couldn't imagine coming into her powers without someone to guide her.

Kayla's story made Scarlett feel a whisper of emotion, one that she quashed ruthlessly. The teen was too thin and her eyes look bruised. Kayla's color rose high as she pushed Lilith behind her.

Scarlett was surprised to see the protective side of Kayla. Kayla had been a loner all her life, and had no friends. This had Tia's love written all over it. Living here had changed Kayla. She'd come a long way from her stint in juvie.

The attic wasn't a musty, dust-infested storage area. It was an impressive hangout space for Tia's foster kids and Magnolia. There was a music area with a large sound system in one corner, along with a few instruments hanging on stands. The far wall had a small stage. A basket overflowing with costumes rested against the curtain. But what really caught her attention was the artwork pinned up on the walls. "Magnolia's getting really good at painting," Scarlett said with a touch of awe.

Kayla's expression was wistful. "Yes, she has."

Scarlett smiled briefly, then returned to more pressing matters. "Tia do you have someone to work with Kayla on the I-think-therefore-magic-happens situation?" Scarlett asked.

Her sister looked fierce, far more protective than Kayla. "You come in here, take over, and have the nerve to ask me if I know how to help a teen witch control her powers? How dare you."

"Since I've already tried to civilize you youngins with sweet tea, I'm gonna withhold baked goods for a whole week if you don't find and use your manners." Sophia's expression was serene, but there was steel behind her words. "That means you too, Tia."

"Yes, Mama. You're right." Tia took a few cleansing breaths, and a couple more before she apologized. "Scarlett, I'm sorry for snapping at you. I may be on edge, but that does not excuse my behavior. I know you were just trying to help."

Scarlett crossed the room, took her sister into her arms, and gave her a squeeze. The hug reached deep into Scarlett's soul, soothing places that were perpetually raw. She had forgotten what good felt like. Scarlett reluctantly released her sister.

She then focused her attention on Kayla. "I know you have Agnayi to show you how to harness fire, but you need someone patient to help you with your involuntary spell casting. Someone who can safely teach you how to control it and potentially use it." Her heart went out to Kayla, who had reverted to hiding behind her long black bangs, which were the length of her short, jagged hairstyle. There were too many powers floating around this room, enough to make a Zen witch wary.

"We haven't had someone mysteriously manifest in quite some time," Tia admitted. "I'd have to check around and see who lives near enough to be helpful."

Scarlett didn't have the luxury of time, and neither did Magnolia. "I can travel pretty much anywhere and have them here in moments. If they don't want to put their lives in my hands, I have the money to send a jet." She wasn't surprised when Tia dismissed both means of transportation. Scarlett grimaced and felt ashamed. She knew exactly how Tia felt about her occupation.

Lilith's thigh-high stilettos jabbed the floor with each footfall, the lethal sound echoing in the quiet space. "I've got money, too, but it's no cleaner than Vanilla Icing's stash." Lilith gave Scarlett a once-over, as if she could tell from her appearance alone the way Scarlett made her money.

Scarlett didn't pimp her body, she pimped her soul, desiccating her humanity one gig at a time. She shook off her morose thoughts so she could focus on the here and now. "Every witch in this room is going to play a role in the rescue. Kayla could be an asset." Scarlett directed her next words at Kayla. She had every right to decide her own fate. "Are you a fast learner?"

Scarlett tossed her a fireball, which the teen caught and quashed into ash. "Well, all right then. I guess I have my answer."

Maxim cleared his throat dramatically. "Are we're done with the Lifetime movie? This is all so very touching, but I have a mirror to enchant. Then I need to go home and feed my pets."

Scarlett laughed. "Your hellhounds Lionel and Felice?"

Maxim's expression softened. He almost looked innocent with his golden blond hair and model-perfect looks. "My demon babies miss Mumsy."

Beau, who had been quiet during this exchange, pulled a sheet off a wall mirror with flourish. "I present to you, from the depths of the Evil Queen's shoe closet, a mirror." He pretended to check his lip gloss in his reflection and tousled his hair, then Beau turned to face his audience. "I think I'm ready for my close-up."

"Good to know the real Beau still exists." Scarlett tossed a gold coin at his feet.

Beau picked up the gold coin and tucked it into his pocket. He winked at Scarlett and bowed. Beau's smile was dreamy and guileless. "Slayers can be glam. Too bad my catsuit is at the cleaners." He pouted. "Scarlett, you wouldn't happen to have a spare pair of leathers? I think we wear the same size."

"Enchant this mirror and you just might earn the right to wear my leathers and a matching motorcycle jacket." Beau was such a goof. Scarlett smirked.

Beau got serious in a fun way. "Chop-chop, Maxim. We have work to do."

Maxim sauntered away from the cluster of witches and back again as if on a catwalk, then directed his comment to Beau. "You betta work!" He waved his hand in an arc and snapped three times.

Chapter Six

Scarlett was always amazed at how simple some magic works. There were no grand puffs of smoke, gurgling caldrons, or spooky incantations used to enchant the gold-gilded mirror. Maxim and Beau joined hands then pressed their free hands on the mirror frame. A few moments of quiet intention were all they needed to wake the mirror.

Beau didn't look back when he spoke to his sister. "No matter how much you want to speak with Magnolia, do not let that wish blossom while the mirror is active. It could be a beacon to the other side and put everyone at risk."

Scarlett put her arm around Tia's shoulders. "If you get tempted, blank your mind. I know you would never endanger this rescue." Magic mirrors were tricky and utterly unpredictable. The one that Maxim and Beau woke was not a portal, but a powerful witch could activate a doorway to another world. The problem with portals was that you were more likely to get sucked into a place you didn't want to be, than to actually reach the person you wished to connect with.

"Show me the events that led up to Magnolia's kidnapping," Maxim commanded in a low tone. It was so close to his I-see-dead-people voice that Scarlett shivered. The mirror rippled, then played the past like on-demand movie.

Tia looked down at her daughter with sad eyes

as they finished cleaning the kitchen. Flour stained the front of Magnolia's apron, and a dash of buttered brown sugar left a smear on her daughter's cheek as she tried to scratch an itch. The kitchen was filled with the mouthwatering scent of Dutch apple pie.

Tia sighed and forced a smile. "Magnolia, you're not talking much this morning. Is everything okay honey?"

"Yeah," Magnolia replied while putting the plates in the cabinet. "I was just thinking about Angel. I feel sorry that I brought Belladonna here, but I hope that everyone realizes that Angel will still be with us. She was meant to be an angel all along." Magnolia's ivory skin seemed to glow, as if she were an otherworldly being. "Becoming a guardian angel was her destiny," she continued, her voice muffled by the heavy refrigerator door.

Magnolia might have been a bit gangly, but she was now strong enough to pour her own milk. A stray tear rolled down Tia's face. She wiped it away when Magnolia plunked the gallon back in the fridge.

Magnolia took a long sip, and then another, nearly draining the tall glass. She wiped her milk mustache with the back of her hand, then picked up where she left off. "Angel will be back to help us when the time is right. But for now, she has lessons to learn on the other side."

Tia pushed a lock Magnolia's hair behind her ear and looked at her daughter with surprise. "You knew she would cross over, honey?"

Magnolia looked directly into her mother's eyes and replied, "Yes, Mom. Angel was here to teach Kayla how to trust." Magnolia pulled her own dark red hair into a ponytail. "Once she fulfilled that duty, it was time for her to cross over. But we can't tell Kayla that now.

She needs to heal."

Kayla gasped. The color drained from her face. Scarlett was tempted to comfort her, but Lilith beat her to it. Kayla's soft crying was breaking Scarlett's heart. Tia's eyes were so glued on the mirror that she missed the mothering moment.

"...and she would never see Angel's passing as anything other than her fault." Magnolia walked over to her mother and gave her a good long squeeze. "This is not your fault either. You have to believe me, Mama."

Tia nodded in agreement as she tucked Magnolia's head under her chin. She kissed the soft curls as a few tears slipped down her face and onto her daughter's hair.

Magnolia pulled away and made a funny face. "Growing up isn't so bad, Mama. I'll always be your baby."

"I know." Tia couldn't help the shuddered sob that escaped her lips.

Her young daughter smiled enigmatically as she deliberately changed the subject. "Lilith will lift her spirits, but her heart is still fragile. She won't be able to see the beauty and love in what Angel did for her. She would only turn it into another reason to hate herself. So, this will be our secret, okay?"

"Sure, honey. I'll do what you think is best." Tia reached out and gently rubbed her daughter's angular face.

"Mama, let's go sit on the porch and have a chocolate chip cookie," Magnolia said, as if realizing that Tia needed to feel her baby girl's spirit one last time.

Tia walked over to the cookie jar, grabbed two huge chocolate chip cookies, and replied, "Sure thing, baby. We have lots to talk about."

The two walked out to the porch and chatted

about everything and nothing, just enjoying each other's company.

The air around Tia and Magnolia grew thick and rippled like a mirage in the desert. The mother and daughter looked at each other as if they sensed the shift in energy, but their concern was short lived. They continued eating their cookies and laughing.

Magnolia cuddled close to her mother. "Smells like rain," she said, her voice caught in the stage between childhood and womanhood.

Maxim reached out telepathically, so only Scarlett could hear what he had to say. *Inside Magnolia's mind, see through her eyes. You will hear her thoughts and feel her emotions, but only as an outside observer.*

The sensation was jarring, and Scarlett bit the inside of her mouth to quell the desire to control the vision. It felt like someone had taken her spirit and crammed it inside her niece's head. It was cramped and everything inside her wanted to rebel. *If you don't chill out you're going to transcend time and forever be in Magnolia's head,* Maxim warned.

Scarlett took a steadying breath and trusted Maxim. Her next impressions were not her own. She was riding her niece's mind.

Magnolia felt a glow blossom in her chest. Change was coming, but she wasn't afraid. The air was cool against her face. The smell of freshly cut grass and wildflowers usually calmed Magnolia's spirit, but the earth felt…wrong. Out of the corner of her eye, she saw an odd shadow. It moved like dark smoke, in the pattern of a tribal tattoo. Magnolia's heart sped up and even though the smoke moved slowly, she didn't have a chance to put up her shields.

A man appeared in between her last breath and

the next. He had her in his arms before Tia could get ahold of her. Her mother screamed in horror and Magnolia did her best to fight the man's grip. When that failed, she turned into a human flame. Her fire magic didn't even make the evil man grimace. To her horror, she realized that he was immune to her powers.

Magnolia's sight shifted, as if being tugged back into a tunnel. The circle of light, the real world, and her frantic mother on the porch were drifting farther and farther away. Panic blossomed deep in her heart as her body seemed to shift and shrink.

Magnolia was screaming; she couldn't help herself. She was falling, always and forever falling. Her arms reached out, but there was nothing but dark. The man that stole her wasn't rough toward her. He didn't need to be. His magic kept her in his grip. She saw a pinprick of light. As it grew closer, her body hurt as if she was being shrink wrapped. She could barely breathe.

Magnolia was sobbing when they landed in the garden. She wanted her Mama, and didn't like the bad man who took her.

"What the..." her captor cried out as he looked at her. "What happened?"

Another man appeared in the garden, but he didn't walk toward them. He had just stepped through a liquid silver circle that shimmered like water. He was a bad man, Magnolia was sure of it, and that made her cry even harder.

Scarlett wanted to tell her not to cry, but she quashed that instinct. She had no desire to be permanently trapped in her niece's head. So she just watched, and tried to remain calm.

He was tall, with wavy dark hair that brushed his shoulders. The man's ice cold gaze scared her. Magnolia *knew he was going to yell. She braced herself; Magnolia hated people yelling. The man was not happy and glared at the one who had stolen her. "Boa, this cannot be my granddaughter. What have you done?"*

The man set Magnolia down gently, then bowed. He stared at the ground while he spoke. "Master, I swear, she was a girl of ten when I took her from her mother's arms."

The bad man was furious. "I will see you in my throne room within the hour." Giovani spoke softly, but his anger was very loud. Boa stood up and tried to run away, but he tripped.

Magnolia started to go after him. "Are you hurted?"

Scarlett was taken aback by her niece's toddler body and childish language. She had no idea what could have wrought this change. Passage between worlds didn't normally cause a shift in form, age, or speech. And Scarlett had plenty of frequent flier miles. Maybe the aging curse worked differently in the Dark Realm.

Giovani's next words stopped her in her tracks. "Let him go little one. He deserves a scrape or two."

Magnolia sobbed. She missed her Mama. The tall man's eyes changed from cracking ice to a calming blue. When he picked her up, his warm energy flowed through her. Magnolia knew he was a firestarter, and she felt his spirit as it healed and soothed her. She stopped crying and looked up at him in wonder. "You's got fiwer magic like me. More like me than Kaywa. Why your magic feel like mine?" She wiggled her fingers and sparks floated from her palms like fireflies. She giggled, then got sad again. "Why you did have the mean man take me from Mama? I been good."

"You've done nothing wrong Piccolo Angelo."

The man smiled down at her, and she smiled back.

"What's a pickle angel loaf?" Magnolia asked innocently, making Giovani chuckle. Magnolia got cross. She didn't like being laughed at.

"It means 'little angel' in Italian. It's a language your soul is quite familiar with," Giovani confided.

There was something in the way he was talking. Magnolia could tell he was misbehaving. He wanted her to use her big girl voice, he wanted her to age. He couldn't trick her, since Mama told her not to believe strangers. "Why you bein' naughty? I can tell you are bein' bad."

"Not so, little one. I wouldn't lie to you." He smiled warmly. "I'm your grandfather."

"I don't have a Papaw. Mama said so," Magnolia protested.

The man looked unhappy. "She was just protecting your grandmother. When she left me, she wanted to start a new life, so I let her go." He walked over to the bench by the rose bush, and encouraged her to sit beside to him.

"Nana Fia is Demi's," Magnolia stated simply. Demi was her grandma's girlfriend. She didn't have a grandpa.

He nodded. His face was shadowed with pain, so Magnolia took his hand in hers. "Don't be sad."

He smiled immediately, making Magnolia smile big too. Giovani's voice was quiet as he continued. "I miss her and your Mama. They asked me to stay away before they traveled to the Earthly Realm."

"Why they make you lonely?" Magnolia, apparently even in three-year-old form, was still sensitive to people's emotions.

"They wanted to live on the Earthly Realm and I

didn't." Giovani plucked a pink rose and handed it to her.

"Oh this flower is so vewy purty." Magnolia was delighted. She loved flowers. Her smile didn't last long. "Why you take me from Mama and Nana Fia?"

"The Darkness. There was a bad man and a bad woman hurting people. When they took Angel's life, I knew you were in danger. My daughter and her mom are wonderful people, but they can't protect you from those demons." He took a deep breath and changed the subject. "You can call me Nonno, which is what Italian children call their Papaws. If you are not comfortable doing so, you may call me by my given name, Giovani."

Magnolia thought for a moment and realized he was telling the truth. He was her No-no, she could tell by his magic. "I call you No-no. When I go home?"

Her No-no's smile disappeared. She knew he was thinking up a fib.

"I would bring you home right away if it was safe, but it is not." He took her little hand in his. No-no's skin was slightly darker than hers, as if he was in the sun a lot. "I have to find the bad guys first then make sure your home is safe. Once it is, I will return you to your family."

Magnolia kicked her legs back and forth as she touched the rose petals. "Can we call Mama, and let her know I okay?" She hoped so. Her Mama got really scared the last time she disappeared.

No-no slowly shook his head. "If I do, the bad guys will follow my magic and come for you." He stood and dusted off his pants. "Let's get you to my home. There are a dozen chocolate chip cookies, hot from the oven, just waiting for you."

Magnolia clapped her hands happily. "Oh, I loves cookies."

Chapter Seven

Maxim clicked his fingers twice in front of Scarlett's face. She blinked but was woozy. Being in someone else's mind always gave her a headache. She pressed her palm to her stomach. She would not hurl. Not in front of Lilith, that was for sure.

She glanced at the mirror as it went dark, like a cell phone going into sleep mode. Her ears were ringing. Scarlett gripped the nearest bit of furniture, which was a mistake. The rocker knocked her off balance. Beau steadied her.

Tia was the only person still looking at the mirror. Her body was rigid, and if Scarlett was in control of her faculties, she would have predicted what came next.

Tia turned around, her eyes were red and tears were slipping down her cheeks. "You!" she cried out. "You show me just enough to break my heart, but kept my baby's thoughts to yourself. I deserved to see the *whole* thing. You selfish, conniving bitch." Tia slapped Scarlett across her cheek. "How dare you, how dare you!"

The red welt rose quickly. Scarlett tasted blood inside her mouth. She wasn't surprised that her sister recognized the signs of mind riding. The slap, on the other hand, was completely unexpected.

Sophia was a blur of swirling hippie skirts. The outrage wafting off the older woman snapped the thread holding Scarlett's consciousness between the past and present. Her cheek was throbbing. She glanced in the full-length mirror beside the small stage. The handprint was a vivid red against her pale white skin.

"Young lady, you may be too old for me to tan your hide, but—" Sophia gathered herself before continuing in a quiet voice that always spooked Scarlett as a child. "You are an adult. We do not strike each other in anger." Sophia swept her hand in the direction of three shocked teens. "And you have shamed yourself in front of your children." Kayla shrunk inside herself, hiding fearful eyes behind her dark black bangs. Lilith's mouth was open wide enough to catch flies. Luke looked deeply disappointed, as if his favorite sports star was caught juicing.

Tia looked at the hand she'd slapped Scarlett with as if it didn't belong to her body. "I...I don't know what came over me. You know I don't strike people, Mama. Not even as a child." She backed blindly away until her skirt caught on the rough wooden beam on the far wall.

Sophia pulled no punches. "Well you picked the wrong time to start, young lady."

Fresh tears washed down Tia's cheeks. Shame and horror warred for supremacy on her flushed face.

"Maxim, will you be a dear and give these teenagers some refreshments?" Sophia asked in a softer tone. "Lilith, you can even make some high octane coffee, just be sure not to give any to Kayla. I don't want to see how her new powers mix with caffeine."

"Come on darlings," Maxim invited. "I can conjure up any confection in the book. You name your poison and I will swill it to ya." The teens followed him like chicks after a mama hen.

Once the door was firmly closed, Sophia returned

her attention to her only daughter. "Explain yourself."

Tia stammered, but was unable to mount a defense. Her face crumpled in response to her mother's censure. "I'm so sorry Mama."

"*I* am not the woman you owe an apology to." Sophia seemed to loom larger as she unraveled her anger. "Your sister has arrived on *your* doorstep, to help you. She has given you hope and a plan to rescue sweet Magnolia."

Each word seemed to strike Tia straight in the heart. She gripped her chest as if to soothe it.

"You may not agree with what she does to earn her keep in this world, but she has been honorable."

The temperature in the attic was sweltering. Scarlett was amused to discover she, a fire witch, was sweating.

"I know, Mama." Tia started to explain, but Sophia stopped her in her tracks with a wag of her finger.

"Maxim left his cave to come here and help bring our little girl home. He let you see Magnolia, so you could be at ease." Sophia shook her head in disbelief. "He showed you she was safe. In gratitude you question his judgment and hit Scarlett hard enough to crack her skull."

Beau wrapped his arm around his mother's waist. "Mama, can we give Tia a moment to collect herself?" His green eyes were as soft as moss as he regarded his sister. "She needs to work out what she's done and why she's done it."

Sophia patted his shoulder and kissed his temple.

The tenderness seemed to go right through Tia. She was unable to choke back the sob.

Scarlett walked up to her sister, who flinched

when Scarlett touched her shoulder. "I won't hurt you Ti-tia. You take some time to yourself, and come down when you are ready."

Tia's lower lip was trembling. She tilted her head in agreement. The movement caused more tears to fall.

Scarlett produced a cloth tissue and handed it to Tia.

Tia crushed the fabric in her hand, but didn't use it. "Thanks," she rasped.

And just like that, Tia was on her own.

The sobs that could be heard through the closed door tore at Scarlett's heart. She wanted to rush in and make it all better.

Beau tugged her hand lightly, and soothed, "I know, I know. She needs time." His smile was sad. "She's earned this breakdown."

Scarlett watched Sophia descend the stairs as she and Beau shared their moment. Once she was out of sight, Scarlett gave in to her own tears. Beau held her. "Shush, darlin'. I got you."

Beau was the only person she would openly cry in front of, she loved him that much. "Good," she said around the lump in her throat. "Thanks, B."

Beau pressed a kiss on the top of her head. She sagged against him, indulging in this calm before the storm.

"Any time darlin'," Beau promised. "Any time."

They were on the second landing when the front doorbell rang. "Who the hell could that be?" Scarlett asked as she dabbed away the last of her tears.

Beau's face went blank. He seemed to be somewhere else, possibly checking the front door with his mind. "Oh my, this could be trouble." He crossed the hallway and took the stairs too quickly. He stumbled on his own feet, but managed to maintain forward momentum with a firm grip on the banister. "Mama, come meet me at the door."

Sophia moved faster than you would expect for a woman in her sixties. They reached the front door at the same time. Scarlett hung back and braced herself. She set a protective shield around Beau and Sophia.

"Why it's just Winter Casey. Why'dya go and scare me like that?" Sophia was about to open the door when Beau stopped her hand before it reached the knob.

"Not sure if we have a blessing or a curse on our doorstep. Mind yourself." The air currents around Beau were disturbed as he set his own shields.

Scarlett thought this was bizarre. What could be so scary about a social worker? Winter was not just any social worker, she was also Tia's best friend. "Beau, I need to know what to expect."

"The child with her, she could be dangerous." His eyes were glowing as he let his magic flow.

"Well that's helpful," Scarlett quipped. She sent out her own feelers to sense the magic and assess the threat. There were no weapons or shields of any kind, and not a trace of malice. Maybe her half-brother was a bit high strung. Beau was prone to fantasy and drama, after all.

When Sophia opened the door, Scarlett was absolutely certain that Beau was off his game. Winter was elegant as usual, with a simple cream blouse and navy trousers. Her wool jacket was open and she wasn't carrying any weapons. Beside her was a slip of a girl, so slender that she was barely more than skin and bones. Scarlett mentally scanned her for magic, and what she found was useful, but didn't ring any alarm bells. The child could see dead people just like Maxim, but she wasn't evil.

"Sorry to drop in on you like this, Sophia. I tried calling but Tia didn't pick up her cell." Winter was so earnest and lovely she would fit inside a historical novel of any century. Her shoulder-length dark hair was flawless and smooth, just like her fair complexion. "I have an emergency placement." Winter gestured toward the child at her side. "She got expelled for graffiti."

Sophia's soothing presence seemed to steady those standing just beyond the threshold. "Well, that hardly sounds like grounds for dismissal."

"I'd thought so, too, But it was the subject of her graffiti and the scale of the artwork that tipped the balance." Winter turned to the child. "Is it okay if I share a picture of your work? I promise they won't get mad."

The girl had the most fascinating blend of features: light brown skin with a generous smattering of freckles across her nose. Her eyes seemed to hint at Asian ancestry, and her lips were the only full feature on her entire body. She couldn't be more than five feet tall. There was nothing dark or sinister about her. Scarlett had a few marbles knocking around in her head from mind riding and her sister's brain rattling smack, but no matter how messed up she was feeling she could recognize danger. Her life often depended on it.

Sophia's expression was soft and welcoming, the epitome of a kindly grandmother. "Can I see your artwork?"

The girl's light brown curls bounced as she nodded her head.

Sophia took Winter's smartphone, but didn't

look at the photo gallery right away. "Where are my manners? My name is Sophia, what's yours?"

The girl spoke just above a whisper, as if she was afraid of Sophia's response to her name. "Pandora Price."

"Oh that's a nice, strong name." Sophia woke the cellphone's touch screen, and what she found shocked her so profoundly that she dropped it.

Scarlett reached out with her energy, caught the phone before it could hit the floorboards, and called it into her hands. Her fingers shook as she scrolled through the images. She blanched when she saw a panoramic view of the bathroom wall. The portrait of Magnolia was so real Scarlett expected to hear her young niece's childish babble. She was sitting next to Giovani, holding a pink rose.

Chapter Eight

Winter looked so confused. Pandora was trembling and tried to hide behind Winter. "I thought that it might do Pandora some good to meet Magnolia."

Tia walked down the stairs. Scarlett could tell she had taken the time to clean up. Her face was freshly washed and her thick curly hair was tamed with an elastic band. She had on a pair of well-loved jeans with a somber green tunic. "Winter, I need to speak with you a moment. But first things first. Pandora, my name is Tia. This is my home and even though us adults might be acting a little funny, you can stay here the night." Tia sounded like her old self, but the sadness in her eyes lingered.

"Beau, can you see if Kayla has time to go to the tire swing with Pandora?"

Kayla spoke for herself. "Pandora, there's a play area outside. I know you are a big kid, but the tire swing is lots of fun. We can even take turns."

Scarlett was impressed, first that Kayla was able to sneak up on her, and second that she was getting better under her own steam. Scarlett was wary of Pandora. Beau could be right about her. At the same time, this kid needed a home. She could relate.

Beau joined her at the foot of the staircase, as if Scarlett had called him. It was eerie how well they were connected. She murmured so only Beau could hear, and protected her words so that none of those with psychic abilities could listen in. "Beau, go out and keep an eye on them. Make sure they don't go near the places where Kayla has had problems in the past. You might want to cloak yourself so Kayla doesn't feel like she's being watched."

Beau nodded. "Pandora, my name is Beau. Tia and Scarlett are my sisters, and this lovely older woman is my mama." His smile was warm, even though mentally he was on high alert. "I wish I could stay and get to know you better, but I have some work to do. See you around, 'kay?"

Scarlett resisted the desire to smirk at the irony of Beau's words.

"Kayla, thanks for stepping forward." Tia looked proud. "You're the newest one to the house, so I figured you could show Pandora the ropes."

Kayla's face brightened, as if this new responsibility was a gift rather than a chore. "Sure will. Pandora, why don't we see if Lilith wants to play too?"

Smart move, Scarlett thought. It was easy to forget how tough and street-smart Kayla was. She'd had a hard life before moving here. Scarlett could already sense the chemistry between Pandora and Kayla. Lilith had been lurking in the hallway, and was about to follow right behind the girls when Scarlett called her over.

Lilith gave her the stink eye, but complied.

"Lilith, I need you to be the bodyguard, but you need to be subtle." Scarlett took a book from the shelf beneath the staircase. It had been one of her favorites, and she knew it would appeal to Lilith. "Read this, sit by a tree off to the side, or anywhere you please within fifty yards of Kayla and Pandora. Now I need you to be calm for the next thing I have to say."

"Whatever, Yoda. Speed this up before they get too far ahead of me."

"Beau thinks this girl could be dangerous, but I'm not sure how."

"Are you fucking kidding me? Kayla's been through enough." Lilith's pale cheeks were flushed with anger.

She reminded Scarlett of Harley Quinn, from her punk pigtails to her lethal, sexy sense of style. Though she would probably slit the Joker's throat if she had a chance. Lilith was dangerous, too.

"Protect your girlfriend. I know you wouldn't have let her out of your sight anyway. Go on."

Lilith probably resented the order, since it was something she had already planned to do. There was one thing for certain: Lilith wouldn't let anything happen to Kayla. Between her and Beau, Kayla was as safe as someone could be in times like this.

The grandfather clock chimed four times. The air felt oppressive, as if the house was holding its breath. The lurking threat of violence and dark magic had Scarlett on her toes, but she didn't have time to worry about what *could* happen. Scarlett needed to be present, and in the moment.

Sophia excused herself so she could get started on dinner. "I need to keep an eye on Maxim. It's my kitchen and my castle, after all."

Scarlett chuckled. Sophia gave her a kiss on the cheek on her way to the kitchen. Tia looked hurt. Withheld affection could be painful. It had turned her brother Rayne into a bitter, vindictive creep.

Her attention was drawn to the front doorway, where a very uncomfortable Winter was shifting from one foot to another. Scarlett knew the best friends would need to talk privately, but she couldn't grant them the luxury of talking without supervision. "Tia, why don't we head into the meditation space? It's easier for me to shield your conversation from those we don't want listening, and I can protect you both as you talk."

Tia surprised her by saying, "Good idea. I might need to let my guard down, and I'd feel safer if you had my back." Tia looked uncertain. "That is, if you want to join us."

"This is about family. There is no place I would rather be."

Winter was the last to enter the meditation space. Scarlett did her thing while Winter and Tia got comfortable. "This house is too quiet, is Magnolia on a play date?"

Chapter Nine

"Magnolia isn't on a play date, she's with Father." Scarlett was impressed with how steady her sister's voice was.

Winter crinkled her cute nose in confusion. "Magnolia's father?"

Well this is interesting. I wonder if I'll finally find out who he is? Her sister wasn't feeling generous with her past, but she did bring Winter up to speed. Each new detail added to the obvious distress on Winter's face. She was a bit too posh for a social worker, but not precious. Her office was as worn down and rickety as the cubicles of her co-workers. She was there because she cared, not for the paycheck.

"So you are sure she's not in danger?" Winter asked as she plucked at the pleat in her slacks.

Tia's laugh was shaky and sounded wrong. "No, I'm not."

"How can I help?" Winter had no magical abilities, but she was kind and resourceful.

"Tia, would you mind if I made a suggestion?" Scarlett was not accustomed to asking permission, especially not regarding something tactical, but she did because her sister was so near her breaking point. The time they had spent together today was more than they had in all the years since Sophia left Giovani.

"Go on ahead, Lettie." The jab at her hated Southern nickname was a good sign.

"I don't imagine you have much free time on your hands, but it might be nice to have another adult around."

Tia tilted her head in surprise. Scarlett smirked; she was glad that she hadn't become utterly predictable. "There's a lot going on, and I think Sophia would feel better if another magic-free adult was here to help her wrangle these teenagers."

Winter brightened, her skin was aglow with purpose. "I'd be happy to. Besides, I think I have about twenty months of vacation time on my hands."

Scarlett's eyebrows raised.

"I'm exaggerating, just a little." Damn it if Winter didn't make her heart beat faster. What was it with her and older women? "Plus it would burn Agatha Burbalm's butt to have to fill in for me."

Tia chuckled. "Maybe we should rig the office with cameras. That video would be viral in no time."

"The old dust bucket will have to deal." Winter's smile lines crinkled beside her eyes and lips. "I'll let people know to call me in an emergency, that way someone who really needs help can find me."

Tia hugged her best friend. "Thank you. If you are feeling really brave, you can stay in our guest room." She winked at Scarlett. Thankfully Winter didn't see the embarrassing gesture. Scarlett could only imagine the razzing she would get once Winter left to gather her things. She wouldn't even fight back. Teasing Tia was better than Desolate Tia.

"Oh, a sleepover and Sophia around to cook, too! Count me in."

Scarlett zoned out as the other women made arrangements. The wood and cushions in the room held the scent of incense. Love and peace was a living presence in the meditation room. There was a shrine off to the side with flowers floating in a bowl and unlit incense sticks nearby for rituals. A copper singing bowl and ringing stick was set on a bamboo mat, next to a large woven basket that held at least ten yoga mats.

Demi, Sophia's girlfriend, was the yogi master. She was an Earth mama that complimented Sophia's hippie style. The *sannyasi* didn't have conventional magic, yet Demi's presence lingered. Scarlett was tempted to roll out one of those mats and stretch though some yoga poses, but there was no time for that.

It was clearly hard on Sophia to have all this going on without the support of her partner. But she was the one who urged Demi to leave, even though it was so close to Angel's memorial. Demi's trip to Tibet had been planned for months and the people she would be staying with didn't have access to modern technology, not even telephones. So she couldn't exactly ring her up and ask her to come home.

Scarlett was getting restless and there were things that she needed to do that were more pressing than chaperoning this heart to heart. "Tia, why don't you two catch up with each other? I'll leave the protective wards in place. You text me when you are done." Scarlett wasn't actually giving them privacy. She'd hear every word, even if she left the property, but they didn't need to know that.

"Thanks Scarlett, for everything." Her sister looked so vulnerable, but it wasn't Scarlett's place to fix it. Tia had Winter for comfort.

"Anytime, sis."

The kitchen was mostly empty. Luke was reading in the breakfast nook, while Sophia was whipping up what looked to be an impressive dinner. "Expecting the cavalry?" Scarlett asked.

"Kinda." Sophia winked. Mother and daughter looked so alike that it made Scarlett's heart twinge. "Could you spare a burner for a potion? I think Luke's about ready to drop his bruiser chic look."

Luke perked up at the prospect. "Really? I thought you said they would never heal." He winced. Talking was obviously still painful.

"Actually, I know the snake that bit you, and I have a few special ingredients that will fix you right up." Scarlett realized she was starting to sound like the Southerners in the house. She couldn't help that she was a natural mimic. In fact, it was one of the things that made her shape-shifting so convincing. She could not only look like someone else, she could sound like them. But more importantly, she was able to temper her magic so she could project the aura of the practitioner she was pretending to be. She scrawled out a list of ingredients. "Sophia, this is your kingdom, and I wouldn't want to mess up your system. Do you have the things I need?"

"Yep, everything except the special sauce." Sophia didn't need to be told what the secret ingredient was. She was the best cook in the house, and that included potions. Sophia didn't have the magic to make the spells work, but she was a great guide—invaluable to untrained witches and masters alike.

Scarlett leaned in so that only Sophia could hear her. "Ya know, I could go get Demi for you."

Sophia tensed, then let out a long sigh. "She's been planning this trip to Tibet for about as long as we have been together. I couldn't bear to take her away from her pilgrimage."

"Even with what's going on? She might be mad at

you for not fetching her."

"Be that as it may, I feel that she is safer off the grid than she would be here. Demi will have plenty to contribute when she returns, and I suspect we'll need all of her healing support."

"Good point. Let me know if you change your mind, 'kay?"

Sophia kissed the top her of her head, and gave her a squeeze. "You always were a good kid."

Scarlett left the embrace as soon as was possible without seeming rude. She couldn't afford to get used to these hugs.

Back on task, she focused on crafting the potion to heal Luke. The special "sauce" that Sophia had alluded to before was Scarlett's blood. The reason the healers in the house failed to cure Luke was that they didn't possess the key ingredient. Without the cure, he would slowly waste away and die of blood poisoning. Rayne, the weakest link of all of Giovani's children, had cast the spell, and only blood magic could break it and lead to a full recovery. Sophia, Terrance, and Memaw didn't have that blood connection, so their efforts were futile from the start.

Scarlett worked quietly, sure to stay out of Sophia's way. Sharing a burner was a big deal. Very few people got the privilege of sharing Sophia's domain. She left the room as the ingredients simmered.

When the bathroom door clicked shut, she faced it and put a protection spell on the wood. She scanned the area for any traces of dark magic before she opened a vein and let a few drops of blood drip onto a small scroll that held the healing spell. She placed it in a vial and corked it.

Scarlett scanned the room again to be certain no

blood had gone astray. Her blood was not only potent, but presented a risk. Even a drop could be used to craft a poison strong enough to kill her.

Sophia had been keeping an eye on her potion. She did it without being asked. "Thanks." Scarlett dropped the vial, cork and all, into the black iron pot. The brew seemed to inhale the last ingredient. The final product was pungent and thick as molasses, but wouldn't taste remotely as good. She poured the viscous concoction into a clean vial, then nodded toward the empty pot. "Sophia, can you put a blowtorch to that?"

"Sure thing, honey. Now step away from my stove. I've suffered your presence long enough." Sophia used a special cleaning fluid that would purge the ingredients and render any remnant of Scarlett's blood unusable.

"Luke, lead me to your bedroom. This stuff is going to knock you out cold, and I refuse to carry your bulk up the stairs." When she looked back, she was amused by the blush on Luke's face. The tragic prince had a crush. That could be useful.

"Is this going to hurt?" Luke asked as they took the back stairs to the second floor.

"Would you like it to?"

Luke groaned. "What is it with you women?"

Scarlett's laughter was deep and throaty. She decided to stop messing with the boy. "It won't hurt, but it will taste terrible."

"What was the secret ingredient?"

Apparently, the lad had been listening. "Dirty socks."

"Oh good. I thought it was going to be something gross."

She laughed again. "I like you, kid."

"Lay off the 'kid' stuff. You're younger than me."

"Point taken." Scarlett opened the last door at the end of the hall. "Now lie down and prepare yourself."

Luke obeyed without comment. Once he was tucked in good and tight, she handed him the vial. For some reason this felt intimate to Scarlett. She guessed in some ways this was; there was literally a part of her in the potion.

"Oh my god, you did put sweaty..." Luke was out cold before he could lodge any further complaint. She rested her hand above the angry bruises on his neck as she murmured the spell verse. Scarlett focused her attention from the crown of his head to the soles of his feet to remove any lingering injuries from Rayne's attack.

"Good night, sweet prince." She kissed his forehead. That wasn't a part of the spell, but it felt right.

She turned toward the windows and was about to set a protection spell when she heard a young child squeal. Scarlett pushed the curtain aside. There was nothing sinister going on. Pandora and Kayla were just having fun. The latest foster child in the house didn't feel evil, but the best spell casters could conceal their true nature, even to her. "I hope Beau is wrong about you." She didn't need another dragon to slay.

Chapter Ten

Kayla couldn't believe her eyes. Tia, peacemaker and supermom extraordinaire, had hit Scarlett so hard she'd nearly knocked her off her feet. After everything they'd seen, Kayla felt just as awkward as Luke and Lilith. The air in the kitchen was stifling. She wasn't in the baked goods mood either, no matter how talented Maxim was at conjuring them. Besides, things had gone so far off script that she needed time to sort things out.

This day had been so cluttered with drama she felt nauseous. Lilith had forced her to snap out of her funk, then kissed her. Moments later, Tia opened Kayla's bedroom door so forcefully the knob dented the wall.

The news of Magnolia's kidnapping made her world tilt. Her first memory of young Magnolia had been a vision where she was taken by a woman with long black hair. *Probably Belladonna.* Magnolia's fake imaginary friend was a demon. That demon had made Kayla watch as she slit Angel's throat. Angel was Kayla's first and only true friend.

Everyone had been so careful. They all knew about the premonition and still it happened. Kayla was convinced she was a curse from the moment she walked into Tia's group home. The one thing that wasn't her fault was Tia's attack on Scarlett. After that horrible red handprint blemished Scarlett's albino skin, she thought for sure Scarlett would have retaliated, but she hadn't.

Kayla heard Scarlett's conversation with Beau, even though they were two flights up. Her hearing had sharpened while she mourned Angel. Kayla found it hard not to cry when she heard Scarlett sob.

The doorbell rang, and Kayla's heart kicked up a notch. She left the kitchen in time to see Beau's bizarre behavior. He had been a court jester up until this point. Powerful magic on him seemed like a shoe that didn't fit right. One thing was clear: whoever was on the other side of that door could change everything.

The child with Winter looked harmless and completely terrified. She was like a younger version of herself when she first moved in, gaunt and starved for love. She wanted to run up and protect her.

Kayla needed out of this house. Her faith in Tia was shaken, but this child needed her. More importantly, she did not trust Tia with this girl, but apparently, that feeling wasn't mutual.

Tia didn't see her in the shadows when she asked, "Beau, can you see if Kayla has time to go to the tire swing with Pandora?"

Kayla spoke for herself. "Pandora, there's a play area outside. I know you are a big kid, but the tire swing is lots of fun. We can even take turns." She felt Lilith's eyes on her as she guided Pandora down the hall and into the kitchen. Even Kayla had feelings for Lilith, there was no doubt in her mind, but she didn't need someone watching her every move—it felt too much like juvie.

She knew excluding Lilith would cause more tension. Pandora was as skittish as a kitten trapped in a drainpipe, and one wrong move, or in her girlfriend's case one stray bolt, would permanently taint this experience. Kayla wanted Pandora to feel at home, the way Tia had made her feel on her own first night. Kayla's heart seized. She had thought her days with violent foster parents were over.

"Is the tire swing meant for, well, someone taller?" Pandora asked, helping Kayla shake the ache in her heart.

"Actually, it's a safe size for a preschooler, but not too small for us to have fun." She made sure to keep an even pace, Pandora was at least a half foot shorter than Kayla, and looked like she would snap like a twig if she tripped.

"Why is the scary blue girl staring at us? She looks real mad." Pandora was trembling slightly as they reached the play area.

Kayla gave Pandora a lopsided grin. "She may look scary, but that's because she's protective of me. The past few weeks have been hard."

Pandora calmed a bit, but she was wary. "You look skinny like me and you're dark beneath your eyes. Are you sick?"

Kayla sat down in the tire swing, her legs long enough to keep still as she answered the girl's question. "I was very sad and I haven't been eating much."

"I eat so much, especially after I draw, but it doesn't seem to stick." Pandora tugged at her baggy hoodie. "Adults don't believe me. They think I'm throwing up after I eat." She grimaced. "Totally gross, I would never. Besides, what ten-year-old starves themselves? I love food." She tugged at a loose thread at the hem of her hoodie. "I had one foster mother follow me around after I finished eating."

"That must have been fun."

"She even got her *true* daughter to watch me at school." Pandora pressed her lips together until they were pale white. "I don't like anyone in the bathroom with me, ever."

Kayla swayed in the tire swing, alternately bending and straightening her knees. Her eyes were on her new black high-tops. "I don't like people in the bathroom with me either."

Pandora plopped to the ground. Turns out she wasn't fragile. "Why?"

There was a secret Pandora was hiding, a big one. It was like a beacon to Kayla, but she wouldn't ask something she wasn't willing to explain about herself. "All the doors here have locks on them, including the bathrooms. So you don't have to worry about anyone following you or seeing something private."

The color drained from Pandora's light brown skin. Kayla had hit a nerve and regretted it. She decided to change the subject completely. "Look at me, hogging the swing. You wanna give it a go?"

Pandora looked relieved and was soon in the tire swing. She did her best to keep her thin body in balance. Kayla was stricken by how slight Pandora was; if she were an adult, Kayla would worry about anorexia. It wasn't the symptoms that bothered her, it was the secrets behind the grasp for control. Kayla didn't want to think about what someone did to Pandora to make her not eat. Kayla had some dark memories of a past she didn't want to share. *She said she eats. Stop judging her. Not everyone is a liar.*

"Can you push me? I'm a little too spread out to get going on my own."

"You got it." Kayla pushed as hard as she dared, making Pandora squeal with delight. She found herself laughing, caught up in Pandora's simple joy.

She was having fun up until when she spotted all her watchers: Lilith fake-reading a book, Beau trying to be invisible, but the one who worried her most was Scarlett. *Why does happiness always seem to make Scarlett so damned sad?* Kayla wanted to wave her over and invite her to play. Scarlett had secrets too, and they weighed her down.

When their eyes met, Scarlett let the curtain go.

I guess spending too much time in the light makes her feel her darkness.

Chapter Eleven

Winter arrived at the house shortly after Kayla and Pandora came in from the backyard. Scarlett was impressed to see that Winter had packed light. She only brought a small suitcase and a valise for her laptop. Sophia fussed up a storm, helping her move into the guest room and get comfortable.

Winter felt a family meeting was in order. She took the chair next to Tia to lend her best friend some support, while still being emotionally available to the foster children, especially Pandora.

Lilith sat between Kayla and Pandora. Her arm rested protectively on the back of Kayla's chair. Her expression was stormy. She cut a few sharp looks in Tia's direction as she maintained her vigilance.

"I apologize for my unforgivable behavior. I know I have let you all down." Tia sat at the head of the dining room table. Her hand trembled as it rested on the placemat. "Scarlett, there are...I'm sorry."

Scarlett didn't let her sister waffle long. "I accept. You're not used to being the center of the tempest and you lost your cool." She placed her hand over her sister's to help center her. Their hands were completely different. Scarlett's skin was so pale it was nearly translucent, her nails were pared down short, and there were signs of past battles, scars that no healing magic could erase. Tia's complexion was peaches and cream, with a generous helping of freckles. Even though her sister's appearance was quite youthful, her hands showed the hallmarks of middle age.

Scarlett may act older than her chronological age, but her skin was smooth and unlined, as you would expect from a teenager. "Tia, the reason why I was the one to hear Magnolia's thoughts was because I have emotional distance. It would have been impossible for you to repress the desire to stay with Magnolia. That would put everyone in danger, on both sides."

Tia looked like she was going to object, but stopped herself. "I understand that, but can you tell me why she arrived there as a toddler? I thought the aging curse was irreversible."

Maxim cut in. "Scarlett may have been privy to Magnolia's thoughts, but neither of them had any idea what was happening or what to expect."

Scarlett was frustrated by her lack of insight. "She was being protected, of that I am sure, and that act of grace may help us to understand what Father wants from her. Kidnapping her was a huge risk." Her bun felt too tight. She let her hair down and fluffed it out. She didn't miss the blushes her unintentionally appealing gesture inspired, but chose to ignore it. "What could he possibly want from her? It's not like he could turn her."

"Running out," Pandora said. "Marker's running out. Sophia do you have another blue? I'm almost finished." They had decided to let Pandora be present in the room and let her draw. It seemed to calm her.

"What are you drawing?" Sophia asked as she produced a second set of markers.

"The way in," was her simple reply.

Scarlett shuddered as if someone had walked over her grave. "Pandora, can I see it when you are finished?"

Pandora didn't look up from her drawing, but she did answer. "Um, yeah, but it might be confusing to you."

Scarlett couldn't help herself. She got up and joined Pandora at the breakfast nook. "Can I watch while you draw?"

"You already are."

She chuckled. Pandora was a cool kid. She had expected to see another portrait in a pretty setting. Instead, she found what looked like the inner workings of an electrical panel: wires, computer chips, and even the vague imprint of a hand. "Why did you put a hand in the middle of the panel?"

"Oh, well, that's how the lock works. The door only opens if you press your hand." She rested her hand in the middle of the drawing. Her fingers were stained with different colored markers. "My hand is too small, but I know how to make it seem the right size."

Maxim was at Pandora's side so quickly the air ruffled her hair. "Oh dear God. I know why she's here."

Pandora met Maxim's eyes. "I belong here?" She looked pleasantly surprised. "Most people kick me out when I draw."

"You are a very, very special girl." Maxim wasn't the type to be in awe of anything; he was one of the most jaded people Scarlett knew. "Scarlett, she can open Magnolia's door." He directed his next comment to the artist. "Pandora honey, you drew the lock, but do you really think you can open it?"

"Yeah, I can open just about anything." She seemed excited to share. "The first house I got kicked out of was when I took apart their security system. I was only four. I ran out of markers and was bored.

They got very mad at me."

"Hot damn." Maxim was nearly glowing with excitement.

"We can get my baby back?" Tia seemed ready to put on her traveling clothes.

Maxim leaned back and crossed his designer-clad feet at the ankle. "Not yet."

Sophia rested her hands protectively on Pandora's shoulders. "Tia, she's a child. A very gifted child, but still young. We can't bring her into Giovani's castle."

"She is not a toy or a weapon." Kayla's voice was hard. "Don't let your own needs blind you. Her life is just as precious as Magnolia's. You told me natural born or not, you love us all. Or were you lying?"

The room seemed to hold its breath.

"You're completely right Kayla. She's not even decided if she wants to stay. Pandora, even if you were the only thing between me and getting my Magnolia back, I would never use you that way." Tia seemed to draw strength from her own words. "Maxim, can you help me understand what Pandora's artwork means?"

"There may be a way for Scarlett to use what Pandora knows, without putting either of them at risk."

"How the heck will I manage that? I'm good, but Father is more than capable of keeping me out of his suite." Scarlett was getting frustrated. A flutter of sparks surrounded her, until she tamped them down.

"Whoa!" Pandora said in amazement. "You can pull stuff through the air and be a sparkler. Way cool!"

Scarlett chuckled. Leave it to the new kid to help her lighten up.

"Being in the land of milk and honey seems to have made you forget your profession." Maxim waited a beat and when Scarlett failed to follow his logic, he continued. "You can make your magic feel like the one you are pretending to be. If Pandora teaches you well enough, you can break in and Pandora can be safe and sound, on this side."

Scarlett grinned. She had been on the Earthly Realm too long. "Good point. But there is a more pressing issue to address."

"Which is?" Maxim had his hands on his hips in full-on gay boy mode.

"Either Chewbacca is hiding under the table…" She checked dramatically. "Or Kayla and Pandora's stomachs are crying out in stereo."

Pandora laughed. "I had Chewbacca for lunch. Maybe he's back to life in there." She rubbed her tummy.

Everyone laughed.

"Sophia, get these two something to eat, stat." Scarlett made believe she was checking for signs of life from Pandora's stomach. "If she can eat Chewbacca whole, none of us are safe."

Chapter Twelve

They may not know who reversed Magnolia's aging spell, but there was one thing for sure: it wouldn't be permanent. Each time her niece spoke with words that matched the age of her soul, her body matured. Her grandfather had known that, probably counted on it, but what could he get out of her aging? His evil motive didn't matter. If he wanted her to age, Scarlett was going to stop him. Making the potion and breaking the spell was the first offensive act of war, one that should come off without bloodshed.

Scarlett wished she knew who cursed Magnolia. The recipe for breaking the aging spell should work, but having the blood of the person who set the curse would guarantee its effectiveness. She left the house after a few stilted goodbyes.

Scarlett was looking forward to some peace and quiet, and the Deadlands suited her fine. No one came here. Despite its name, things did grow in the tainted earth—dark things, deadly things. There were scars on the trail, blast marks on boulders, and desiccated trees sucked dry of life. The Deadlands was a training ground for demons, and a dueling ground for idiots who wanted to risk death in the name of pride. They fought here. Father would never allow dueling that was not designed or decreed by him. He would decide who lived or died in his kingdom.

Some of the seeds and dreary ingredients for

Magnolia's potion were fossilized. Others trapped in amber or tree sap. Scarlett loved the overbearing silence and the aura of death here. It was far more relaxing than the rollercoaster of emotions swirling around her sister's house. There were some witches that were more interesting than others—the Bloodthirsty Beau and the Erratic Lilith. "Wanna dance?" Classic. She and Lilith would have been friends in high school for sure, if she had been permitted to go to high school in the first place.

"Actually, I would love to dance. I haven't been in flesh long enough to attend a ball." Belladonna's voice was silky like Italian chocolate.

Scarlett moved on without acknowledging the woman who had callously murdered young Angel to steal her life force in order to return to the flesh. She conjured a 3-D topographical map and consulted it. The map wasn't a true one, and neither were the red coordinates marking particular locations.

Her heavy booted footfalls contrasted with the click-clop sound of Belladonna's heels. *Heels. In the Deadlands. Is she fucking kidding me?* Scarlett didn't make a comment. It would be fun to see Belladonna fall on her ass and dirty her skirt. She didn't look back, but was mildly curious as to what century Belladonna's clothing would be from—the formal gowns from the time period from which she was banished, or the current day chic.

Scarlett continued to ignore the woman, which elicited some colorful curses in Italian. She wondered if she kissed her mama with that mouth. That mouth. Scarlett sighed. The sentimental thought spurred her to tackle uneven terrain, riddled with ruts and shell casings. The dark trees cast lurid shadows in the wan moonlight.

Rank air and the stench of death didn't wrinkle her nose. She was used to the evil residue. The sound of high heels fell away as she climbed the embankment along a dry riverbed. It was a relief. She didn't want to talk to Belladonna and it had nothing to do with Angel. She had never known Angel, but unfortunately she could not say the same for the shape-shifting demon stalking her at the moment.

Scarlett shuddered as a ghost form walked right through her, embedding expensive French perfume in the cilia within her nostrils. The bitch hazed right through her. Scarlett froze.

Soon the haze reformed to reveal Belladonna. She was achingly beautiful. The stunning demoness wore an elegant burgundy dress with a mermaid silhouette. She was a softer, more beguiling version of Sophia Vergara. Her slender face had delicate features, but it was her full, sensuous lips that mesmerized Scarlett. Mentally, she shook the fascination and silenced her arousal. "Sleeping with me won't put you back in my father's good graces."

"You were always vulgar, like an uncut diamond." Belladonna moistened her lips and parted them. "A little polish would reveal something of value."

Scarlett resisted the desire to grind her teeth. Immortal femmes may look like young women, but they all acted like mothers. Scarlett didn't need a viper like Belladonna as a mother. She already had a demon mother, thank you very much. Vivian, the one who birthed her, was a succubus and an assassin. If her mother caught Belladonna sniffing around Scarlett, she would burn the demoness from the inside out. The pain would be endless.

Belladonna reached out and traced her manicured nail along Scarlett's angular jaw. "Some nights, you were more like a shimmering opal."

Belladonna's touch was more intense now that she was of flesh and blood rather than a spectral presence. Even when she had lacked a definitive form, her touch had been intoxicating. Especially for Scarlett's younger naïve self. Fifteen was too young for any child to be sucked into a torrid affair.

"I don't need sonnets from you about my albino features." Scarlett stepped out of touching distance. She wanted to scorch the nail that touched her skin, but refrained. She had things to do. "Shouldn't you be wrapped in the arms of your beloved, rather than trolling around in the dark woods with me?"

Belladonna drew closer and rested her hand on Scarlett's forearm. "You used to find my love pleasing. Why do you spurn me?"

Scarlett walked away and counted to ten. She would love to wield a death that would stick, but she didn't have time to cover her murderous tracks. This was a waste of energy. If she was delayed much longer, her father would sense her presence and command her to his throne room. "I'm not going to lift your skirts, so stop wasting your wiles on me. If you persist, I will put you in a cage and leave you here."

Belladonna was not deterred in the least. "You've been on the Earthly Realm. I thought I could join you when you return."

Scarlett's laughter was bitter. "Oh that's rich, you want me to—" Scarlett finally got it. Belladonna couldn't travel between worlds. She idly wondered who blocked her passage and trapped her here. She walked within kissing distance, then sent out her magical feelers.

Belladonna's pupils dilated; she was clearly aroused. Her breathing came in delicate pants. The shallow rise and fall of her breasts was appealing, but Scarlett's focus would not be swayed. "Father has trapped you here. Now all this makes perfect sense."

Belladonna put her arms around Scarlett's neck and tried to kiss her. Scarlett gently removed her hands, regretting the way her body reacted to Belladonna's intoxicating perfume and dark aura. "I'm not fifteen. That won't work on me anymore."

Anger flared briefly in Belladonna's eyes, but she quickly quashed it. She cast a mesmerism spell to seduce Scarlett, but it bounced hopelessly off of Scarlett's protective shields. "If you don't leave willingly, I will kill you for sport."

Belladonna stepped back, fear replacing the beguiling expression on her face.

"When I kill a demon, they stay dead. A thousand slain innocents couldn't secure your freedom from that fire." Scarlett was getting angrier. She didn't have time for this shit. She waved her hand, casting a spell of her own—a magical LoJack, as it were. She would now know where this deceitful, cunning bitch was at all times. She lied about the spell's reach. "If you don't leave, and stay far away from me, your youth will slowly leach from your flawless body." Scarlett raised her hand and a ball of violet grew on her palm. "Ready to be a crone, Belladonna?"

Belladonna took another step back. Terror glistened in her tear-filled eyes.

"You stay gone, or you will be a hag in minutes. There is no antidote for that, either." Scarlett's smile was bitter. "No one would ever want you again. Ready for that final shape-shift, *darling*?"

Belladonna disappeared before Scarlett's poisonous threat was complete.

"Now where was I?"

Chapter Thirteen

"I always hated that bitch, especially when she toyed with you for sport." Vivian's smooth voice was impossible to resist, especially for her prey. Thankfully, the mesmerism didn't work on those who shared her blood.

Seeing her mother was the icing on the cake of a truly fucked-up day. "If it helps, I don't think she's going to be around long."

Vivian was dark: dark hair, dark eyes, dark clothes. She was dark in nearly every way, but her skin was nearly as white as Scarlett's. That one delicate trait often disarmed her targets. "If you do plan to kill her, be sure to invite me."

"So you could drink her soul?" Scarlett wasn't being sarcastic. Souls were her mother's sustenance.

"Unless you want to. It would be a shame to let it go to waste." Vivian's black hair shimmered blue in the murky moonlight, the layers were as rich as raven feathers.

Wonderful, two lethal femmes in a row. I guess I'm just that lucky. Scarlett leaned against a tree. This might take a while and she might as well get comfortable. "How may I be of service?"

Her mother's smile was more a baring of sharp white teeth, not unlike those of a vampire. "Your lesser brother has finally done something right. Or wrong, depending on your point of view."

Rayne was at the center of things. His interference incited this war. "Was the assault on Tia's children for Father's benefit?"

Vivian ran her stiletto nails along a tactical baton. She wasn't threatening Scarlett. She liked being prepared to maim or murder—it was one of her few charms. "He thought so. Rayne overheard your father when he was speaking with Jet and Onyx."

"My murderous cousins."

Vivian smiled. "They're so cruel. I wish they were mine."

Scarlett had heard this before. It stung up until the point when she no longer wished to please her mother, which happened at the tender age of six.

"Giovani mentioned his desire to have young Magnolia on this side."

"Did he say why?"

Vivian arched her perfectly sculpted eyebrow. Her mother was shrewd, but didn't push for more information. Vivian had her own agenda, and would probably file this interest away for future reference. Knowledge was power, after all. "He would have, if your brother had bothered to cloak his watery presence. Rayne should have drowned at birth rather than poor, sickly Ophelia."

Vivian didn't seem to care that Giovani chose another concubine. The shine on his evil tarnished over time. She had left him out of sheer boredom. Ophelia had the misfortune of conceiving Rayne. Instead of giving Giovani a fire-wielding heir, she drowned during childbirth. Rayne's water magic filled her lungs to bursting. She was dead before he fell into the hands of the royal midwife.

"He heard what Daddy Dearest wanted, and

decided to go after it. I'm not sure how Belladonna and Xavier got into the mix." Vivian holstered her tactical baton. She was rolling a Chinese throwing star over and under her fingers in the way that humans did with a coin. Even if her fingers slipped, her skin was not vulnerable to sharp blades.

Scarlett rubbed her face as she thought this mystery through. "Jealousy."

Vivian rolled her eyes. "How pedestrian. I understand ensnaring Belladonna, but bringing Xavier...why would he want to include competition for her affections?"

Rayne had always wanted to play with Scarlett's toys. When they were kids, they were literal toys, but after puberty, Rayne lusted after her powers—including her power of seduction. Scarlett found it very creepy that her bother wanted to bed her lovers.

There were times when her mother had the attention span of a gnat. She had put the Chinese star back in a leather pouch. Vivian flicked a butterfly knife open and closed. "Belladonna is clever, but her carelessness with Tia's kids has put a price on her head."

"What's the bounty?" She hated Belladonna so much that she would assassinate her for free. In practice, Scarlett never gave freebies. She just enjoyed certain jobs more than others.

Vivian sighed as if the truth pained her. "A fortune. One your moron of a brother thinks he is going to collect on."

"Is Father going to murder him as well?" This was bound to happen. Rayne lived his life trying to please Father—a fruitless effort. He was a disappointment before he took his first breath.

Vivian finally stopped her deadly weapon manipulation. Scarlett was relieved. This meant that her mother would be leaving soon.

"Not yet." Vivian reached into her leather purse to retrieve a letter sealed with wax. The royal signet had been pressed into the burgundy wax while it was still hot. "An engraved invitation. Apparently, Giovani wants you to visit and stay a while."

Scarlett repressed a smile. She had been puzzling on how to deliver the potion to Magnolia without being seen. Now she had an invitation to stay. It was dangerous, and she liked it. "What a pleasant surprise."

She broke the seal and read the letter. "Oh my God. I'm being cordially invited to a performance."

Vivian's grin was wolfish. "I haven't seen an execution in quite some time. Whatever shall I wear?"

Scarlett tapped the thick stationary to her lip. "Something you won't mind being bloodied."

"Oh that goes without saying. Perhaps I should wear white. The blood castoff would be artistic, like a Jackson Pollock painting." The whites of her mother's eyes voided. They glistened like sinister black marbles. Scarlett guessed she was walking through her closet in her mind, figuring out which dress would look best with fresh blood. Sometimes, Vivian was her kind of crazy.

"I'll have to change. This is the only thing I own that doesn't have bloodstains," Scarlett said with a smirk. Jet and Onyx would certainly be the executioners, but Father may let her take part in the final touch of Belladonna's permanent death. "See you there, Mother."

"I'm off. I only have a week to find the perfect thing to wear." Vivian paused, then produced a parchment from thin air. At first glance, it looked merely like aged vellum, but it was made by something far more disturbing than wood pulp alone. "I almost forgot. This will help you break the aging curse."

Vivian hadn't forgotten a thing, she was just being dramatic. "This ingredient holds a powerful secret, one that Tia would never willingly divulge."

Scarlett took the page from her mother. It held within its fibers the caul from Magnolia's afterbirth. Caulbearers, babies born with the amniotic sack intact, were known to be able to see into the future. The caul was a sign of a powerful witch. "Mother, how long have you known the identity of Magnolia's father? Not even Giovani has been able to figure that one out."

"Trade secret."

Scarlett flashed a smile. "Have fun, Mother, and thanks for the special delivery."

"Anything for my murderous daughter." Vivian meant it as a compliment. Scarlett smiled. Her mother wasn't so bad after all. At least she was predictable, unlike the new Tia.

Chapter Fourteen

Her trip back from the Deadlands was uneventful. Scarlett rode up the steep incline leading to her home hidden in a dark cliff. The location wasn't top secret, but the lack of trees and high altitude made it easy to spot unwelcome visitors. And of course, there were the hazards and snares on less traveled routes to her home. Collecting and creating booby traps was one of her hobbies.

Once her Harley was tucked into the garage, Scarlett entered her home and was not surprised to see her cousins playing video games in the living room, or what the boys sarcastically called her man cave.

"Hiding from Uncle?" Scarlett asked. Jet and Onyx gave their typical response to such a silly question: they grunted in unison and then went back to playing their video game. Although technically they never looked away from the screen, both of her young cousins were keenly aware of her presence, which was to be expected from the experienced warlords even if they were only twenty- and sixteen-years-old, respectively.

No one ever got to be young on this side, at least not in her family. Unfortunately, this was true for her temporarily pint-sized niece Magnolia. She would make a great queen one day, fearsome and fair. Too bad Giovani would never live to see her promise become reality. The truth would break her poor father's heart, Scarlett thought with a little more than a dash of sarcasm and cynicism, but he would never turn Magnolia or be able to use her for his games. Magnolia's caul seemed alive in her leather satchel, as if the magic was trying to agree with Scarlett. She mentally set a protection spell on the parchment so that her cousins wouldn't become aware of its banked powers.

She waved her hand at the flat screen and the game froze. The two sullen young men turned her way, though they would never give her a dirty look. Her cousins would both be dead before a smart-assed remark left their lips. Her house rules had very different consequences than Tia's. The boys didn't live with her, but they hid out here to get a break from the constant vigilance of their uncle and their positions in his army.

"No one has visited?" Scarlett asked, though she knew the answer. She liked to test Jet and Onyx from time to time, to see if they were lying to her. They knew even the mildest untruth meant they could never return for respite, not only from their uncle, but also from their warmongering father, Pyron.

"Nope, not a one," Jet answered, his voice as deep and dark as his soul. The older of the two, he was the one who handled interrogations.

Scarlett nodded, then took the steps up to the main living area. She turned when she got to the landing and cast a spell that would seal her space so not even the combined forces of Giovani and Pyron could break in to her inner sanctuary.

She went into her office and cleared off the long table she used to look at maps and blueprints. Scarlett rolled out a thin sheet of linen to protect both the table and the parchment. According to longstanding tradition, the amniotic sac of a baby born with its caul was pressed against paper. The caul would release from the child and remain on the page. In the case of a child of great magical significance, the caul was not only kept, it was protected within the fibers of the paper it was drawn onto. Now there was a mere shadow of the former shape of the caul. Its magic was still intact and Scarlett was in awe of the power it radiated.

Her hand hovered above the parchment and she asked it for the name of Magnolia's father. She smelled pine needles and maple sap. Scarlett felt the sensation of running, though not with human legs. She was too low to the ground for that. The yips and howls told her what she was and confirmed the identity of Magnolia's father. "Lykos." Her father was not a wolf nor was he a werewolf. Lykos was a tracker. He was the only son of Giovani's biggest enemy, Alessandro Nike.

"Well, shit." Tia couldn't half-ass her rebellion, she had to go all out. No wonder she kept his name a secret. Lykos taking Tia's virginity and leaving her with child would have started a war. One far more bloody than the rescue mission they had planned for Magnolia.

Scarlett got back to business. She'd sort out the baby mama drama later. She put on a set of latex gloves and used a small scalpel to cut a portion of the thick page. Scarlett used a pair of tweezers to place the precious material in a small vial. She corked it before tucking the key ingredient into her leather pouch, along with the other materials for the potion that would break the aging curse that held Magnolia's spirit captive. She put the remainder of the paper in a folder and locked it in her safe.

Scarlett needed time to think about the repercussions of her discovery. When she got to her bedroom she stripped off her clothes, released her hair from the tight bun, and walked into her en suite bathroom.

Scarlett looked in the mirror, as she always did, waiting for the moment that her hard living showed on her face. Scarlett wanted to hold off on using her glamour and shape-shifting powers for anti-aging purposes for as long as was possible. She furrowed her brow, squinted, and even smiled to see if her skin would immediately return to its smooth youthful appearance. She smiled grimly when nothing was amiss. Jet and Onyx would laugh their asses off if they thought their big, badass cousin was vain.

Scarlett rested her hands on the sink and leaned into the hard marble surface. Lykos Nike. Of all the people her sister could have slept with, did she have to choose the baddest boy in the Dark Realm? "How did she manage to meet him? It's not like he was free to roam in Father's kingdom." There were so many questions she'd like to ask Tia, but unraveling this mystery could put their rescue mission at risk. They needed to keep this from Lykos and his father Alessandro at all costs. As for the secret ingredient to break the curse, no one other than Vivian needed to know.

She turned on the faucets in her massive spa shower, then started to brush out her hair. She kept it as long as her sister's curly red mane, just past her waist. Once the last snarl was brushed from her long white tresses, she walked into the spray of water. Scarlett had chosen not to add a door to the luxurious shower. One, she wasn't modest. Two, fogged glass could hide an assassin, she knew this from experience. Her methods of murder always informed how she set up her personal space.

But just for this moment, she wasn't an assassin,

a protector, or a spy. She was Scarlett, enjoying the simple pleasure of warm water cascading down her firm body, soaking her long hair and washing away the ugliness she was privy to on a daily basis.

She pressed a button on the tiled wall and soft music played. Scarlett turned to face the shower wall and twisted the knob, spigots spraying luxurious soft water on her chest, stomach, and knees. Once her skin was flushed, she adjusted the knob, turned around, and moaned at the pleasure of the pulsing water melting away the stress from this long-ass day. She pressed another button at her side and the chamber filled with light steam and the fragrance of sandalwood.

Reluctantly, she left that little slice of heaven and turned on the fan, which sucked the moisture out of the room so she wouldn't break a sweat while drying off. She didn't bother blow drying her hair, she just brushed it out and wound it into an elaborate bun.

Scarlett walked into her closet, past her bad-to-the-bone duds to the rarely used elegant section. She chose sleek tuxedo pants that flared slightly at the bottom, along with a plush cashmere sweater. Scarlett groaned when she realized she'd have to wear heels. Father wouldn't expect her to be prettied up for her entire stay at the castle, but he liked when she dressed more like other women at court. So she humored him. Scarlett had a lot to accomplish this week and had to stay on her father's good side to avoid suspicion.

In one suitcase, she packed all the clothes she would need for her stay, and the other held her various weapons and disguises. She could shape-shift to look like anyone, but that expended energy. When economy of motion was key, it was easier to lean on traditional human tools of espionage. She didn't have to worry about her father confiscating her weapons. Being armed to the teeth was expected, and he may require her to work during her stay.

She walked to the dumbwaiter that connected her bedroom to her carport below. The scanner examined her eyes to be sure that it was not only her but also that blood was flowing through her veins. Her palm print opened the pressurized doors with a hiss. Once her suitcases were stowed in the cargo transport, she spoke. "Escalade, silver." The device would shuttle her luggage through a series of channels until it was directly above her car of choice. The keyless entry would open the trunk. *Best valet ever.* The only kind she could trust with her personal items.

She ignored the catcalls when she left her inner sanctuary to pass through her man cave. Once in the garage, Scarlett looked mournfully at her Harley; the helmet alone was out of the question. She climbed into her pimped-out Escalade and buckled in, then opened the console. Scarlett plucked the soft pink lip gloss from its hiding place and applied a light coat, which was the maximum makeup she was willing to wear when off the job. Besides, darker colors would look garish on her albino skin.

She pulled out of her garage and looked back briefly at the cliff that hid her cousins from the world. On the other side of that rock face was the only place they could still be kids. That was a luxury she didn't have, even though technically she was still a teenager. Scarlett shook her head. Soon their actions would make even that modicum of innocence impossible. One day they would cross so far into evil there would be no peace for them, no scrap of happiness to enjoy. That thought made her feel sad for them. But they had chosen their path and, like her little brother, she could no longer protect them. Scarlett hoped that she would never need to kill her own flesh and blood, but in her line of work, along with the stakes of the war that was brewing, the severing of family ties was inevitable.

Chapter Fifteen

She had taken the long way to her father's home rather than creating a portal as a shortcut. She loved the quiet her Escalade provided. It even silenced the roiling sea as she sped by. Scarlett parked in her usual place, next to a false wall that led to a tunnel out of the property. This was helpful for pursuing fleeing targets and for a stealthy retreat. Both were useful while in her father's employ.

A young man walked away from a concealing shadow to the driver's side door and helped her out of the vehicle. She spoke into Jonah's mind. *How did you manage to get this detail?*

"Giovani regrets that he is unable to greet you upon your arrival. May I help you with your bag?" Scarlett smirked. He knew carrying the suitcase with her arsenal was not an option.

"Yes, has Father decided where he will put me?"

He wants to keep an eye on you, yet he never seems to see me at all. This is a great advantage. Once you are settled we need to speak. There is trouble with Tia. He raised his hand to ward off any outburst. It was unnecessary. Scarlett never made a scene unless it was a calculated one. "You'll be staying in the same wing as the guest of honor."

Scarlett repressed a grimace. She hadn't counted on babysitting the soon-to-be-dead demon. "Wonderful. Shall we? I'd like to freshen up." They'd talk about this later, once she was settled and all the weapons not physically hidden on her person were under lock and key. She used a safe in conjunction with powerful wards. Scarlett wasn't worried about theft. Stealing from her was not the best career move. For now, she was too valuable to the family to be insulted.

The castle had many of the hallmarks of the deep past, but it was quite modern, with a backdrop of stone and priceless artwork. Tapestries masked hidden passageways for easy assassination. A kernel of heat started deep in her chest and spread with each twist and turn. *He wouldn't execute the prisoners in front of the child, would he?*

Jonah switched her suitcase from one hand to the other. The subtle signal allayed her fears. Father didn't plan to include Magnolia in the violent display. That was smart. Magnolia was unpredictable, especially since she was a toddler again. *I wonder if her old soul still dwells in her body.*

Scarlett's entire being was flaring with heat. Magnolia was close and she was not happy.

"Giovani put you in rooms next to his. He does miss your company." Her room was on the opposite side of what she knew was Magnolia's gilded cage. She would have to pass in front of her father's door to get to her niece. Scarlett hadn't expected to be on such a tight leash, and she would voice her displeasure to Father when appropriate. The proximity could be a boon, however. Some things were both blessings and curses.

"I see." Jonah rested the bag with her clothing in front of the closed door where she would be staying. There was no need for keys as the door wouldn't open for anyone but Scarlett and her father. She regarded the young boy who would soon leave his tween years behind. His features were nondescript, and a stranger would be hard-pressed to describe his appearance beyond his build and the color of his hair—brown.

Father's greatest error was to underestimate this youth, which would work in her favor on this mission. Jonah was the ideal spy and had been cast in the role of nanny. Childcare duty was supposed to be an insult, a reminder of his lack of physical strength. In reality, he was in the best position to protect Magnolia from those who wanted to harm her and keep her company until it was time to escape.

The door to her sitting room opened for her as she drew close to the threshold. "You can leave my bag next to the fireplace." She would set her gun safe after Jonah left. He was an ally, but no one should be trusted completely, especially not those within these castle walls.

The room was masculine and moody. Dark wood furniture matched the wainscoting and crown molding. The mural on the ceiling showcased a battle scene filled with fire and bloodshed. There was a hidden panel there as well, which was handy if she had to beat a hasty retreat. There were no tapestries on the walls. The hidden passageway could only be opened from the inside, and like the first door, would only open when her magic signature was recognized.

She produced a money clip and peeled off a few large bills. Jonah accepted them, even though he hated taking her blood money. He didn't judge her profession, but that didn't mean he approved of it.

What trouble has my sister gotten into? I've only been gone for one evening.

Jonah's facial expression blanked, but his mind

was alive with displeasure. *She risks us all, visiting the mirror and trying to talk to Magnolia. Her desperation could forge a connection and get us caught.*

Scarlett opened the wine colored drapes and lifted the double sash window, letting air into the room as she schooled her expression. She hadn't been able to disarm the video and audio bugs in the room yet. Giovani wasn't targeting her rooms; every suite in the castle had active surveillance, modern and magical. He also didn't complain when she disabled them. He respected her moxie.

Once she was feeling calm, she faced the young man, noting how his baby fat was giving way to more angular features. She noticed that the white streak he had been born with was now more pronounced and was even obvious at a distance. *The electric sparks didn't faze her?*

No, she stopped touching the mirror after the first few zaps. Now she just talks to Magnolia. His expression softened. *She loves her child.*

Anything else to report? She stepped out of her heels and sat in the leather chair by the window, glancing at the formal gardens. The ivy growing around her window framed its perfect beauty. "When is Father expecting me?"

"Tomorrow at brunch. It will just be the two of you."

Scarlett smiled. One upside of living here was the food. "Oh good, then I can truly get comfortable."

Jonah turned toward the door to her suite. *Tia has no idea what darkness she is messing with. Do you think she will use Pandora to wake the mirror?*

"Goodnight, Jonah." Scarlett didn't have time for this complication. She would set a more violent trap for Tia before she brought the ten-year-old child into the mix. *Thank you for your vigilance. Let me know if the next blast fails to dissuade her. I'm going to have to revoke Beau's access to the mirror. Just in case she tries to sway him.*

The door closed without a sound. She went around the room, amazed at the technological upgrades her father had made and the ingenious hiding places for the bugs. She placed each item in a burgundy chest rather than destroying them. Another compromise with Father. She slid the chest into a lead chamber as she whispered her latest spells. Scarlett had upped her game, which was expected. She left it in place for Giovani to remove. Breaking the spell on the small chamber was her father's version of doing the Sunday crossword puzzle in pen.

Tia had annoyed her. The repeated wishes of a powerful mother would eventually create a link, a link that Magnolia would welcome. There were some betrayals her father would not tolerate, and stealing his biggest prize was one of them. Scarlett was not only putting her own life on the line, she was risking eternal torment. All of this was to protect her niece. If she had to protect Magnolia from her own mother, so be it.

The next time Tia approached the mirror, she would get that dance Lilith had offered Maxim. The pain would be extreme, but brief. Saving her sister from herself would not come without a price. The evil residue would stain her sister's soul, like a paint packet tucked into stacks of bank notes. "Sin is seductive, sister. You will soon find out that you have just as much of Father's blood as the rest of us. Let's see if you can resist your darker instincts."

Scarlett traced a blunt fingernail down the

windowpane, following the path of fresh raindrops. Stealing Magnolia back did not mean Scarlett would return her to Tia. "Hopefully one dance will convince you to back off. Your life may depend on it."

Chapter Sixteen

As much as Tia's behavior pissed Scarlett off, she could understand the temptation. Scarlett's own temptation was something Tia could not be trusted with. Magnolia was two doors down and the power the toddler was giving off would have been frightening in an enemy.

Adrenaline was pumping through her body, risk and riding the razor's edge was a high Scarlett welcomed. The room was cool, just how she liked it. Even in the dead of winter, she enjoyed the cold sensation on her skin. She wasn't immune to the elements, but as a powerful fire witch, her body always ran warm. That discouraged cuddlers in bed, not that she let anyone stay. She wasn't a user, she just couldn't trust anyone enough to let her guard down. Not on this side anyway.

She traded the cashmere sweater and tuxedo pants for workout gear. Scarlett would not use the main hallways. The space where she practiced was not like a hotel gym. Only those of royal blood could unlock the door; it had been charmed to sense *family*.

The hidden pathway skirted her father's suite as well as Magnolia's room. The wall the corridor shared with Magnolia's nursery grew very warm. There was a questing tentacle of magic that flowed through the stone and reached out to Scarlett. Her protective shields intercepted and absorbed the call.

"Ana, Ana, I knowded someone there," Magnolia insisted. She refused to believe her nanny. "Iz fiwer magic, family magic, right there."

Holy shit! Magnolia felt her through the wards around her room and into the magic-cloaked passageway by will alone. Morgana was more of a fuckup than Scarlett first thought. According to Maxim, Morgana had promised Father the wards she set around the room would block scrying and conceal Magnolia's location. She was going to be one dead witch once Father found out.

Scarlett's heart beat even faster. Her hand nearly touched the wall to forge a connection when she realized it was acting of its own volition and responding to Magnolia's tantrum. She grabbed her right hand at the wrist and backed away as far as the narrow space would allow.

"It's not No-no, his fiwer feels mean. Plus it's a girl, I just know it." Magnolia's voice got louder and louder. "She has no colors, but she's like me."

She has no colors, what in the world could that mean? Holy shit! She means me, and she's right—albinos literally have no color. As much as she wanted to stay put and see what Magnolia's magic could do, she strode away. Her footsteps were silent. She moved with the stealth and speed of a jaguar.

She swung the door to the gym open forcefully, nearly knocking out the person on the other side.

"Are you fucking serious?" Rayne growled. "Watch where you—"

Rayne was as colorless as Scarlett, except for the dark circles around his eyes. She wondered if he knew what kind of trouble he was in. "I will break your jaw if you don't watch your mouth." Scarlett advanced into the room and Rayne retreated like the coward he was. She noted the haunted expression on his face. His black tank top was soaked through and he looked like he had lost about twenty pounds of muscle. "You never think, Rayne. Only people of the family bloodline can open that door. Name one of those people who wouldn't happily teach you a lesson for your smart mouth."

"Back off." His voice was softer than his words. "I've been—"

Scarlett's irises swirled like molten lava. It was for show, she wasn't furious. "What have you done?"

Rayne's face lost all expression and his energy seemed to cave in on itself. She was grateful that fear didn't make him produce yellow water. "I—"

Scarlett stopped him before he could spew lies. "You should stick to your quarters or leave." She really wanted him to go home, far away from here. There was a world of pain coming in his future, one she may have to bear witness to.

"You can't order me around, you're not Father." He leaned against the open door. "Besides, I couldn't leave if I wanted to."

Scarlett stepped around her brother, dismissing him without a word. He was a fuckup, but he was still her brother. She might be burying him soon, but she couldn't afford to indulge in softer emotions. She had done that far too much at Tia's. *Maybe that's why Tia was breaking the rules and talking to the mirror.* Softly spoken demands were often discarded or seen as negotiable.

The door reengaged. A quick assessment confirmed that she was alone. Scarlett hissed out the breath she had been holding. "I hope I don't get to do the honors." She'd make sure not to get on her father's shit list because one of her punishments could be spilling her brother's blood. *Hope they have a drain*, she thought cynically. The blood and water her brother would expel as he died could fill the throne room. He may not have been the son Giovani wanted, but he was a powerful water witch. His death throes could release a deluge.

She shook her head. "Not my problem."

The monotony of jumping rope purged all directed thought. She emptied her mind as sweat soaked her shorts and T-shirt. She released her pent up frustration on a punching bag. The boxing equipment had been designed to withstand supernatural strength while still giving slightly like a normal punching bag would.

She was into her second hour of going through *katas* from various martial arts when Jet and Onyx arrived. "Anyone want to spar?" she asked.

Her cousins looked at her as if she had lost her mind.

"I promise to play fair."

Jet seemed to consider her offer. "No broken bones, ribs included?"

Scarlett checked her taped knuckles as if she would find the verdict there. "If you insist."

Both Jet and Scarlett were mixed martial arts masters, so the fighting was fierce. Scarlett appreciated sparring with a worthy opponent. Going through martial arts forms on your own can only get you so far. The next thirty minutes had her muscles humming. Scarlett stuck to the letter of her promise. She broke cartilage in Jet's nose and sprained four ribs, and that was her playing nice. She looked forward to not having to playing nice. Killing wasn't just a profession, it was a passion.

She set his nose with a sickening tweak. "You'll be all better in no time." Bruises and scratches looked especially nasty on albino skin. The grisly appearance didn't match the true damage, and Jet had been through worse. At least they hadn't broken out their *katanas*. The Japanese swords were sharp and unforgiving. "Thanks for the workout, I needed that."

"We should spar more often," Jet's deep voice rumbled. "No one in the army wants to spar this hard. I need to know my weaknesses so I can train properly." The bruises and scratches had already begun healing themselves. It took effort and energy to mend your own skin, but healing your own wounds was a necessity, especially when in battle.

She ruffled his short blond hair. "You have the right attitude. You never let your ego get in the way of your training." Jet turned away to hide his blush. She wasn't liberal with compliments, and often caught her cousin unaware. He wouldn't say so openly, but he craved Scarlett's approval with the same intensity that Rayne wanted Giovani's.

Onyx's fists were a blur as he attacked the punching bag. His technique had improved since the last time they had worked out together, but she wouldn't acknowledge it. Praise had to be sparse to be truly respected. "Onyx, you wanna spot me?"

His face lit up, and in that moment he actually looked sixteen. "Are you going to be here long?"

Scarlett knew he wanted his own shot at sparring, but he was still too green for her tastes. "Giovani has a *performance* for me to attend next week, and has invited me to stay."

"Cool. Hey, um. Maybe we can work out together

again while you are here?" Onyx's voice was as deep as his brother's now that the typical adolescent voice changes were behind him.

The chances that she would contact him were slim, but she didn't want to quash his enthusiasm. "Sure, I'll text you."

His smile was breathtaking and reached his eyes.

"Enough of this chatter. Load up the bench press, and don't go easy on me." The bar nearly groaned under the extreme weight. She enjoyed the burn from the reps. She might even sleep tonight. If the sparkler down the hall didn't drive her batty.

Chapter Seventeen

Mama loves you. I'll be there as soon as I can. Scarlett's eyelashes fluttered. Sleep held her fast.

I know you're alone right now, don't be scared okay? Be brave for Mama.

Her body was still exhausted from the extended workout, but something was calling to her. It was hard to hear, as if the words were spoken underwater.

Giovani won't hurt you, I promise. You just need to be brave and you will be home before you know it.

Scarlett bolted upright, sleep gone. She was in danger. In a flurry of motion, she changed from her bedclothes into leather pants and a black top. She was sliding a blade into her motorcycle boots when she heard the next message more clearly.

I love you, Mama loves you, Tia promised.

Jonah, did Magnolia wake? Scarlett spoke into his mind.

No, an elephant could stomp through the room and it wouldn't wake her.

Make sure she stays asleep as I take care of this fucking link. I can only hope Father is not in his chambers.

I wish I knew.

Aargh! Nothing can be done about it. Watch over her. Use my password if you need to escape to the hidden corridor.

I will protect her until my dying breath.

Let's hope doesn't come to that, for any of us.

Scarlett mentally traveled along the link her careless fuckup of a sister had forged, and astral projected into the space unseen. She sent a bolt of anger that knocked the mirror from its hook and shattered the reflective surface on the attic's hardwood floors. Sharp slivers scattered everywhere.

"Oh no, oh no, oh no!" Tia cried in one endless string of agony. "I didn't mean it."

Scarlett blotted out the connection between Tia's home and her father's castle. Once she was certain the link was fried, she installed a magical surveillance device where the mirror had hung just moments before, then returned her spirit to her body in the castle.

Jonah, has she awakened?

Almost. She mumbled some words as if she was responding to Tia.

Fuck. At least I closed it before the whole castle was clued in.

The air in her room was too hot, so she focused on the heat and absorbed the energy back into her body. Her fancy footwork might have severed the connection, but the rage she expended would be a calling card should Father decide to pay her a late night visit.

When she heard the knock on the door, Scarlett nearly fainted. She did a visual check of the room and found nothing out of place. Scarlett tugged on her leather jacket and zipped it up.

"Going somewhere?"

When she saw who was waiting on the other side, she pulled him in and locked the door. Scarlett went from high alert to exasperated. "If I see one wrinkle in the mirror, I am blaming you."

Jonah set up his own sound shields to be sure they

were not overheard. "She didn't wake and Giovani's rooms are unoccupied. There hasn't been anyone there in hours."

Scarlett made a beeline to the safe that wasn't truly a safe.

Jonah chuckled. "You are the only woman I know who puts their mini-fridge inside a safe."

The soda hissed when she twisted off the top. "Good work. Here you go."

This wouldn't be the first time she was grateful to have Jonah in a strategic position. "Protector and now Mr. Sandman. You're growing up into a fine young man."

Jonah had lived a hard life. His childhood had ended on his first day of school, when his baby brother was stolen from his nursery. Jonah's mother never recovered and he'd taken care of her until she ended her own life. Of course he was the one who found her hanging from the rafters. Scarlett wanted to kill that bitch again for all she put Jonah through.

"That was a long time ago." Jonah's voice tugged her out of the heavy memory. It was a smart move. She didn't need to infuse her newly cleaned room with fresh anger.

"Yes it was." She resisted the desire to ruffle his hair. Extended childhood didn't exist on this side, but she had wanted more for Jonah. "How has she been?"

Jonah smirked. "She's certainly giving Adriana a run for her money."

"Tia Two you mean? Sometimes Father has no sense. Choosing a nanny that looks like the child's mother was a bad move." Instead of bringing comfort, the familiarity would only make Magnolia crave home more. "There is one upshot. She's been using her magic unconsciously without aging."

"Yes she's a chubby-cheeked bubbly terror." He pulled a small compact from his pocket. "Tia couldn't honor the responsibility, but I know you will. You need eyes on her when I am not around." He handed her a smaller version of the mirror Beau and Maxim had enchanted. It was slim, easily stowed, and could pass as a common accessory.

"Brilliant packaging and cheeky too." The silver compact was engraved with the sacred flame.

Jonah was pleased, his cheeks pinking briefly before returning to their natural tan hue. "I upgraded the spell with your latest *crossword puzzle* as inspiration."

It was disconcerting to know how aware Jonah was; as if he could surf the waves of spells all around him without being detected. He was also loyal and true. He loved Scarlett and would never betray her. "You certainly keep me on my toes, but no peeking into my rooms, for spells or anything else."

"I didn't mean to invade your privacy, and I would never—"

Scarlett gave in and ruffled his soft brown hair. Jonah's eyes were a deep soulful brown, like a young buck in the forest. "I know that, and I also know our mental telepathy means you are attuned to me. Have you been cleansing after each meeting?"

"Yes, I empty all our shared thoughts while I meditate. Though I doubt anyone would bother to look. I'm invisible. The only one who sees me is you."

The sadness tugged at Scarlett's heart. He was lonely but never bitter. She admired him. "That's your biggest superpower. We wouldn't have a shot at success without your *cloak of invisibility*."

His smile was wan.

"Rest Jonah, even if only on the cot in Magnolia's nursery." She lifted the compact and promised, "I'll watch over her as you sleep. I won't be able to fall off again. Someone might as well get some z's."

He patted her shoulder and looked at her with eyes infinitely older than her own.

"You did good tonight," Scarlett said. "I trust you to look out for the little one. See you at brunch." She had been a little surprised to learn Father had invited him.

"I'm going to be the help, while Adriana is with Magnolia." Jonah didn't look insulted or upset. He was used to his various odd jobs.

Scarlett was relieved to have him there. He could listen for the subtext behind the words while she kept her own thoughts safe from Giovani. "See you in the morning, Harry Potter."

Jonah's smile was genuine. "Bye." He departed quickly, more like a mist than flesh and blood boy. She was jealous of his stealth.

She sat heavily in her chair. The leather hissed slightly from the abrupt impact. Scarlett closed her eyes and clicked on Tia television. Her sister was on the floor desperately trying to gather all the shattered pieces, but there was no saving either the mirror or the squandered opportunity to see that Magnolia was safe and sound.

Beau drew her into his arms while Sophia tended to the cuts and mirror splinters. They were three shades of heartbreak. *You made your bed Tia.* Soon enough Tia would feel the awakening darkness in her blood. The choices she would make in the next few weeks could mean her redemption or her ruin. "There is no escaping Father's blood."

Chapter Eighteen

Giovani Vulsini was a swarthy man you would expect to be on a pirate ship or a conqueror in the ancient world—both were professions he once belonged to. He looked wrong in a business suit, but Giovani was a man of the past as well as the current day, so he tolerated the clothing that powerful men wore in the twenty-first century. The one thing that he did not abandon was his long wavy black hair and trim beard. Scarlett was a bit amused by the streaks of gray hair, since it was an affectation. Her father was immortal and forever in his prime.

"Greetings, daughter. I'm so glad you could come for a visit." He kissed her on both cheeks and pulled out her chair. She graciously accepted this chivalry even though she would break the hand of any other man, or woman for that matter, who tried to do the same.

"It's been quite some time since we last met."

Jonah came from the servants' entrance and poured them coffee just the way they liked it. The boy had been serving Giovani for many years and not speaking to Jonah was another attempt at humiliating him.

Jonah attended to them with quiet confidence. One glance in her direction let Scarlet know that the room had no prying or scrying audience. The three of them were completely alone. She hated treating Jonah without respect, but making a fuss on that front would only raise her father's ire and that was the last thing that she needed. "Father, as always, I appreciate your hospitality but am confused by my placement in the castle. If you want to know something regarding my whereabouts, you could simply ask or watch me from my childhood suite in the royal wing."

Giovani chuckled. He knew this game and ignored it. "We have a special guest that needs monitoring, someone I would not trust with—"

"Young Magnolia."

Father looked surprised.

"I've felt her magic. She's quite impressive."

Pride washed over his face before it returned to a neutral expression. "She is what Rayne should have been."

Scarlett knew as much. But the question she wanted answered most she could not ask. "I'd argue that she is more than what he should have been. Even as a toddler, her powers far exceed his. She could crush him like a grape."

Giovani's aura changed. Pride mixed with greed. "Hopefully it won't take too long for her to mete out punishment. She is too new. Maybe you could turn her head."

The room grew warmer and she could feel her father seeking her thoughts. She locked her mind up tight. "She's bathed in light and radiates it. I'm not sure I could successfully tarnish her."

Giovani ripped open a fresh loaf of bread and dabbed a corner into the yolk of his eggs. He ate the fist-sized bread as if were a cream puff and not dense sourdough.

She decided to enjoy her food. The waffles were light with the perfect crust. Powdered sugar, softened butter, and syrup were divine complements to the hot delicacy. In normal settings, the waffle would have cooled shortly after leaving the iron, but food in the castle didn't have the same weakness. She bit into a fresh strawberry the size of a plum and reveled in the true sweetness. Fruit in Tia's neck of the woods looked pretty, but rarely had any flavor at all.

"I will not task you with that, at least not directly." Her father devoured what was left of his over easy eggs and was feasting on his ham, sausage, and bacon. When Father let his guard down, he ate like a Viking.

Jonah removed her syrupy plate and served her a massive slice of frittata. The eggs were airy, with a trace of buttery goodness. The savory vegetables were a perfect complement to the cheeses melted into the eggs. "Brunch is one of my favorite events in the castle. Thank you for taking the time to join me."

"You are the only child that has exceeded my expectations." Giovani looked at her in a way that made her feel seen. She often forgot this side of her father. He was proud of her and her accomplishments. "Your stubborn independence may be trying, but I can respect that."

"Thank you, Daddy." For all his evil and cruelty, she loved him. Spending time with Tia, Sophia, and Beau made her feel good, but there was always the unspoken judgment regarding her mercenary profession. It was nice to be on this side and accepted for all of who she was, including her secrets and sins.

He rested his large tan hand on her pale white one. She always marveled at the contrast of their skin tones. Most of the children from his line were albino, with the exception of Beau and Tia, who had fair skin covered in freckles along with improbably red hair.

"Did the midwife ever give you a straight answer regarding our albino features?"

"Irony."

Scarlett laughed a full-on belly laugh. Giovani's dark-magic-wielding children and nephews were completely colorless. "Maybe that is a straight answer."

Giovani joined her mirth. "Speaking of amusing situations, would you like to murder Belladonna?"

Scarlett paused. There were times when she wanted to separate Belladonna's head from her delicate neck, but Scarlet's rage regarding her seduction at Belladonna's hands had cooled over the years. "I would not deny Jet and Onyx the pleasure of executing someone so worthy. Will Xavier die as well?"

Giovani's eyes were a luminous liquid silver. "He will not escape the consequences of his treachery. I haven't yet decided what I am going to do with Rayne, but my tolerance of his disgraceful behavior has run its course."

Chapter Nineteen

Father's throne was a subtle rise with little decoration. The audience chamber had a limited guest list. Vivian was sitting beside him in the throne meant for the queen. There hadn't been a queen in over a century. He just enjoyed having Scarlett's mother close.

Vivian's hair was swept up in a hairstyle that would have been more fitting for an upscale wedding than a beheading. She had gone with a silk sheath dress. It was white and would look deliciously grotesque covered in castoff blood. The only pop of color was her Taylor Swift red lips and the soles of her Christian Louboutins. The stilettos were high and sharp enough to puncture a heart. Scarlett wondered if Giovani would give Vivian the privilege of piercing Belladonna's.

Giovani's suit was solid black from his tie to the tips of his Gucci loafers. His lapels were silk, but the remaining fabric was matte. Her father's shoulder-length hair was the only outward expression of his roguish past. He rose from his throne and strode purposefully toward the woman standing before the platform. "So let me get this straight. You kidnapped my only grandchild, brought her to my realm—in my gardens no less—without my permission?"

Scarlett looked at Belladonna and wasn't surprised to see the defiance in her eyes. She was either suicidal or figured that she was to die and would rather do so with her elegant head held high.

Jet and Onyx flanked Scarlett. The young men looked like white marble statues: cold, flawless, and unforgiving. Tonight they were not her cousins, they were executioners. Scarlett was amused by their clothing choice, or lack thereof—leather pants, boots, and they were shirtless. Vivian wasn't the only one excited by the prospect of a brutal execution. Blood spatter against albino skin would be both lurid and profane.

"Giovani, I was supposed to tempt the child to our side. It was a part of our agreement," Belladonna said haughtily. Scarlett figured being in the flesh for the first time in two hundred years could do that to a girl. They were supposed to kidnap Kayla, not Magnolia. If Belladonna's attitude was any indication, she had no idea this was the case. Father had clued her in on the finer details at brunch. Rayne was in deeper shit than Scarlett had imagined.

The slap echoed like a gunshot in silent chamber. Belladonna's shock was priceless. Scarlett resisted the desire to cheer. Vivian was similarly amused, but didn't conceal her mirth.

"You ingrate!" Giovani shouted. He slapped the bitch even harder in the exact same place the first blow had landed. Belladonna fell to the ground, her hand resting on the hot welt that blossomed on her pale skin.

Xavier was livid, and almost stupid enough to strike his Lord and Master.

"You." Giovani glared at the young man. Xavier's normally tan skin was growing sickly white. "I give you a chance to break the curse and have your wife back, and you dare look at me, poised to strike."

"Forgive me, my Liege." Xavier got down on his

knees and bowed so low his nose touched the ground.

"Belladonna, I would think two hundred years would have made your far wiser. Yet here you are, careless. Again." Giovani walked over to the cowering woman and stepped on her hand, slowly increasing the pressure until he fractured the small bones. The shattered bones pierced the tendons and veins. He laughed while she screamed.

He moved his foot away from her ruined hand, then grasped her by her hair and pulled her to standing. "You even showed your true form to Kayla, in the middle of a schoolyard. Are you fucking insane? You risk us all for a parlor trick?"

Giovani's fury over that particular stunt had not waned. Belladonna had taken over the body of a teenager at Kayla's school, Grace Chandler, the rich bitch with short blond hair. Out of spite, after Kayla's rejection of her clumsy attempt at friendship, Belladonna ran her hands through Grace's short, stylishly mussed do and shifted it to her own long black tresses. She nearly blew her cover, just to be petty.

"What possessed you to imprison Kayla and have her watch her best friend die?" Giovani didn't give a fuck about the teen's feelings, but what he did care about was Belladonna breaking the spirit of a witch he wanted in his army. "Broken dolls are not soldier material."

"We needed her powers to help me cross over." Belladonna whimpered as the hand pulling her hair heated, burning her scalp without setting her hair on fire.

"Lie to me again, bitch, and I will feed you to Jet and Onyx."

Belladonna wilted, the fight in her completely

gone.

"You didn't have to wake her to use her powers." He punctuated each "you" with a cruel shake of Belladonna's head. "You could have left her passed out in the cave. You resented her resistance to your wiles and games. So you wanted to punish her." Giovani gripped her hair even tighter, then went nose to nose with her. "You did so without my permission, and for that I am going to make you pay." He released his grip and grinned slightly at the sound of her head cracking painfully on the stone floor. He left Xavier and Belladonna to stew on that for a moment.

Morgana, the seer, was Giovani's next target. The crone shrank when his eyes bored into hers. "Morgana," he snarled. "You promised me a girl, not a baby. Have you been lying to me, keeping secrets?"

"No...nnnnn-never, my Lord." Morgana was shaking violently. "She was ten in my vision, just as I told Boa. The aging curse on her was so strong." Her sobbing was making it hard to understand what she was saying. "It was unbreakable. Those good witches tried, and failed. I have no idea what happened." Morgana kissed Giovani's feet as she begged for mercy.

At the mention of the aging curse, Scarlett's curiosity blossomed. She quickly quashed her thoughts. She couldn't let anyone in the room know who cursed Magnolia, never mind why he did so in the first place. Truth be told, she had no idea why Lykos cast the spell or what he hoped to gain from doing so. Scarlett locked down her mind. These thoughts were too dangerous in her current company.

Giovani loomed over the crone. "This was your last chance. I was going to lock you in the dungeon permanently, but if you keep on sobbing I'll rip your head off."

Scarlett was impressed with Morgana's sudden silence.

"Guards, bring Rayne in."

Rayne was marched into the room. He didn't resist when they chained him to the wall. For now, he was just a witness.

"Jet, as the oldest, you get first choice." Giovani clapped his hand on the young killer's muscled shoulder. "You've earned it."

Jet didn't speak, he merely pulled Belladonna up by her now snarled black hair. "Two centuries of night will be heaven compared to what awaits you." He flicked his wrist and a weapon appeared. The handle was blunt and encrusted with sapphires. The blade itself was eighteen inches long and cursed. He stabbed her right through her heart and left the blade embedded in her chest.

"Oh my *bella donna*, my beloved..." Xavier's sentence ended in a scream as his wife's blood spattered his face.

Onyx, ever patient, waited for Belladonna's last heartbeat before gathering his prize. He surrounded Xavier, and his dead demon wife, with Greek fire. The controlled blaze licked over the blood, but didn't make it sizzle. The fire simply rested on the liquid.

"Noooo..." Xavier screamed, over and over again. The soon-to-be-dead demon was terrified of fire. He was sobbing and reached out to hold his dead wife's body only for it to be consumed in hellfire. "*Cara mia!*"

Onyx walked through the fire without fear; his own blaze could never hurt him. He gripped Xavier and dragged him over his wife's charred body, being sure to tread through whatever blood that had yet to boil.

Vivian stood close enough to the blood and fire to singe the hem of her white dress. "Sire, can I behead Belladonna? It won't be as much fun as ripping her head off while she lives, but the indignity would give me satisfaction."

Giovani's irises were a liquid silver, yet even in his rage, he thought of Scarlett's feelings first. "Daughter, you are the one she wronged. Would you like to do the honors?"

Scarlett looked at the charred bloody mess that was her former lover. She had no desire to touch Belladonna ever again. "I will let Mother have the privilege. Her soul is still lingering, held here by Xavier. *Bon appétit.*"

Rayne hung from the shackles on the wall. He was as silent as the dead.

"Onyx, execute her pitiful husband."

Xavier's screams were cut off with his head.

Chapter Twenty

"Did I make the right choice?" Scarlett asked. "Yes. Tia won't follow the rules you lay down, no matter how practical. She wants Magnolia back and it's blinding her. Her violence toward you has hurt her standing in the family. She feels she has nothing left to lose."

Scarlett opened the front door to Tia's house and led the way into the kitchen. Angel Villanueva was so petite that Scarlett's body blocked the view of her spirit as they walked through the doorway to the kitchen. The ghost's translucence blended in with her pale-skinned bodyguard. It had been only a few weeks since Belladonna took Angel's life, yet she was already acclimated to being a spectral presence.

"Who the hell are you?" Pandora stood abruptly and put her body in between Kayla and the unexpected guests.

Scarlett added fierce protector to list of skills the unusual ten-year-old had.

Kayla may have been behind Pandora, but she easily saw over her head. "Pandora, you know Scarlett." When Angel walked around Scarlett, Kayla trembled and started to cry.

Pandora repeated her first question as she surrounded Kayla within her cloud of protection.

Scarlett forestalled the pint-sized banishing. "Pandora, meet Angel Villanueva, Kayla's best friend.

She was one of Tia's foster children."

The freckles on Pandora's cute nose crinkled as she tried to digest this piece of information. "Since when are ghosts in the system?"

Angel floated closer to the young girl. "I died—"

"You were murdered," Kayla corrected. Kayla was swimming through so many emotions that Scarlett was growing seasick: anger, despair, heartbreak and above all, shock.

"What was Winter thinking, placing me here? Safe my ass." Pandora maintained her protective stance. "Magnolia's been kidnapped, Angel was murdered, and Tia pimp-slapped Scarlett. Kayla, we need to leave. No good can come of living here."

Scarlett busted out laughing; she couldn't help herself. Pandora's dirty looks gave her the giggles. She was a munchkin with soft curly brown hair and a dusting of freckles on her warm brown skin, but her presence exceeded her age and experience. The madder Pandora got, the harder Scarlett laughed.

Beau nudged Scarlett as he and Winter entered the room. She could feel his amusement, and he would normally put on a show to diffuse the situation, but it probably wouldn't go over well. "Pandora, the world is a dangerous place. Things around this house may have been an unwelcome carnival of emotion, but we care about each other here," Beau said.

"Love doesn't hurt. Tia slapped Scarlett hard enough to leave a welt the size of my head." Scarlett knew she should have healed herself right away. Nothing could be done about that now.

Winter walked to Pandora's side. "You're right sweetheart. It's never okay to hit someone you love."

Angel hopped up on the island with a dramatic

thump. When she was alive, she made a point of showing the world she was a solid and not a gas. Scarlett was impressed that Angel was able to manifest strong enough to impact worldly things with such force.

"I see you've taken over my job as cute Latina," Angel teased, then turned to address Winter. "Good job mixing the makeup in this house. Gotta keep things interesting."

Pandora seemed caught between her desire to throttle Scarlett and to navigate the shifting sands in this household. "I'm not Latina. I'm not anything."

Angel tilted her head, as if she was trying to un-see how Pandora saw herself. "You're not any one thing, that's true. You're just more than us usual folk, a combination of many cultures: Latina, Native American, African American, Asian, and a dash of Irish, hence the freckles." She crossed her eyes comically. "I'm just a boring old *Boricua*."

Pandora leaned back against Kayla as if drawing strength from her older friend. "What's bor-eek-qua?"

"A Puerto Rican." Angel kicked her feet, ever youthful. "Oh, and thanks for not vanquishing me. I've worked too hard to be seen by you warm bloods."

The younger girl laughed. "Kayla's the warmest, she can make fire. But you already know that."

Angel giggled. "She makes a lousy fish though."

Pandora turned to look up at Kayla. "You can't swim? I can't swim either."

"Shorty is talking about something that happened when Angel was alive." Kayla swallowed back the emotion that was threatening to bring her to tears. "I thought you couldn't visit us yet. I miss you."

Angel was fiddling with a spatula. "Normally I'd have to stay away until you accepted that I was gone."

"But you're here now, why can't you stay?" Kayla squeezed Pandora's shoulders gently before walking toward to her first real friend. She plucked the spatula from Angel's hands. "Stop it, you're driving me nuts."

Angel's grin was playful until Tia walked down the back stairs. Tia tripped over her own feet when she saw Angel's ghost. She recovered her footing, but emotionally she looked as shaky as a newborn foal.

Angel hopped down and wrapped Tia up in a big hug. "I love you Tia."

Tia gasped. Tears ran down her cheeks. "I love you too, Sunshine."

Kayla's expression darkened as she observed the reunion.

Scarlett hoped that Tia would be given a chance to earn back Kayla's trust. If she didn't turn her attitude around, one morning Tia would wake up to find both Kayla and Pandora gone. Scarlett didn't know why, but she was sure Kayla would leave Lilith behind. She could feel the punk rock girl sulking in her room down the hall. Scarlett figured she was pushing Kayla away before Kayla could abandon her. *Damn shame. I know they love each other.*

"I'd like everyone to take a seat at the table. Scarlett, can you fetch Sophia and Luke? They're outside in the witch's garden. Kayla why don't you break the Punk Princess out of her domain."

Scarlett saluted on her way out the back door. The screen door closed with a loud clack, rebounding once or twice before the lock clicked into place. The icy breeze blew the dead leaves around the porch. Some of them retained their fall colors, but quite a few were dead brown.

She was happy to see Luke healthy and social.

Sophia was doing a good job building his self-esteem. "Hey, you two. I was sent out to gather you into our little war party, but I need these ingredients before we head in: lovage root, red clover." She double checked the list on her smartphone. "You wouldn't happen to have anise out here too?"

"The last one, is that to protect Magnolia from turning evil?" Sophia asked.

"Yes, it will block the effects of living on the other side. I need some mugwort, got any of that on hand?"

Sophia gave her a look that said *I have everything and then some.* "In the greenhouse. Anything else, bossy pants."

Luke let out a bark of laughter then quelled it.

"Don't stop laughing on my behalf. Contrary to popular belief I do have a sense of humor."

Luke and Sophia had on muddy garden gloves, and various clippings and grasses clung to their clothing. Sophia was a combination of the earth and sunshine. There were fall leaves in her otherwise tidy white hair. Scarlett enjoyed the burgeoning chemistry between the two. Luke even looked like he was at home. Sharing his truth had been good for him.

"The last thing I need is rosemary oil and a place to brew the elixir in privacy. Luke and I need to get the anti-aging potion ready for Magnolia." She had a vial of her own blood in the pouch that held the ingredients gathered from the Deadlands, along with the fragment of the caul-laden parchment. She wouldn't be able to relax until the genetic elements were safely in the brew. "I need a cauldron you won't mind destroying. The stuff we will be using has too much dark energy to be washed away."

Luke's brow crinkled. "We can't use dark magic.

Not on little Magnolia."

Sophia answered on her behalf. "Dark magic wrought this spell, and it will take dark magic to break it. Besides, you survived Scarlett's poison and came out all right."

Luke blanched. "You poisoned me?"

"There are some spells that can only be broken with a mixture of dark and light. Everyone in our family, save Sophia, has mixed blood." Scarlett put the elements Sophia harvested in the pouch fixed to her leather belt. "Luke, you don't mind missing the reunion with Angel, do you?"

"She's back?" His brown eyes lit up like a child given his birthday presents early.

"Yes, she won't leave without saying goodbye, but we have work to do. I can't spend too much time here. Father is expecting me back soon and he can't know what my true mission is." Scarlett figured this was willful ignorance on her father's part. He ignored anything that would show Scarlett in a negative light. She was the great dark hope in the family. No matter how much he liked his nephews, they weren't his children.

Luke trailed her up the path to the house. "What does he think you are doing?"

"Killing a target or two."

"No, really, what did you tell him?"

Scarlett ignited the lava flow within her irises, causing Luke to step back. "I'm an assassin, Luke." Scarlett smirked, then drove her point home. "I make dead people."

Chapter Twenty-one

"Now Scarlett, I thought you had more manners than that. You are as subtle as a jackhammer," Sophia teased as she tapped Luke's shoulder. "How you have managed to stay alive this long is beyond me." Sophia was trying to shake free some of his shock. "Luke, I may not agree with the way Scarlett fills her purse, but she's honest with me and I trust her."

Sophia kissed the top of Scarlett's head and left the two on the back porch. "Go on, say what you need to, ask questions. I promise there will be no deadly consequences." She winked at Luke. "Besides, I just healed you. No need to mess up my own work."

"Sophia trusts you, and normally that would be enough for me, but things have changed a lot since you left." Luke crossed his arms, unconsciously flexing his considerable muscles. He had managed to pack on quite a few pounds. Being back on solids and no longer laid out must have helped. Working with Sophia in the gardens did the rest. Luke was healing himself without knowing it. "I thought I could trust Tia too, but after what she did to you, I don't really trust her anymore."

Scarlett sat down on the top step and tapped the wood beside her. "Have a seat, stud."

Even in the waning light, she could spot his blush. He was kinda cute. The wood groaned a bit under his weight. "We need to reinforce these steps sometime," Scarlett said.

"You make dead wood, too?"

Scarlett grinned at his attempt at humor. "No, I go to the hardware store like everyone else." She was happy to see that he had recovered completely. More than that, she was happy he had found his place in Tia's home—at Sophia's side, in the kitchen and in the gardens. "You know Sophia doesn't just let anybody cook in her kitchen, right?"

Luke grinned. "She doesn't let me touch anything yet. I'm just the stock boy."

"Does the earth talk to you?" Scarlett asked seemingly out of left field. "What about wildlife?"

Luke closed his eyes and focused. A fox sauntered out of the woods and curled up at his feet. After a few moments the fox was snoring.

Scarlett nudged his shoulder, unintentionally catching a whiff of his cologne. Most guys his age bathed in the stuff; she liked that Luke didn't overdo it. Scarlett wished it didn't have an erotic effect on her. Luke's groan of dismay helped her extinguish the thought. "Sorry. I forgot you were an über empath. Speaking of, how are you managing on that front?"

He let out a large sigh. "The first time I woke up after you slipped me that mickey, it was like someone had turned a faucet on full blast. Tia's been too messed up to help me, but I find meditation takes the edge off."

"Yoga and meditation, smart move. Demi must have taught you well."

"I miss her." He looked at Scarlett, the sadness was weighing him down more than he would admit.

"Yeah. She would be a big help with all that has been going on in the house." While Demi wasn't a witch, she had mad skills when it came to spirituality. She could mellow a firecracker. It was a shame that

Sophia's girlfriend was on the other side of the world in Tibet.

"Yeah. I'm about as flexible as a tree stump, but I try."

Scarlett laughed and Luke joined her. Part of her was with him while she monitored the other situation inside. Angel kickstarted the healing process. People were talking with rather than at each other. Time was ticking by, and she needed to get started. "Come on, we have work to do."

It was clear Luke didn't fully trust her, but at least he'd stopped vibrating like a tuning fork. The folks sitting at the dining room table were so wound up they didn't bother looking in their direction as Scarlett gathered what she needed and let the stock boy carry the heavy stuff. She led the way up the stairs so she could scout out the attic before he entered the space. "We're all clear," she called to Luke.

She got the brew going, including a vial of her special sauce. Her blood would activate the spell and elevate its power. She took a good long look at the other vial, the one that contained a fragment of Magnolia's caul. It seemed like such a precious thing to embroil in dark magic, but it was the only way to definitively break the aging curse. Scarlett added anise and mugwart to prevent the darkness from tainting Magnolia's light. Once the elixir was simmering, she dropped another bomb on poor unsuspecting Luke. "Okay, you're up next. Time for you to cast the spell."

Deer in headlights, that was Luke for sure.

"I told you that you would be playing a pivotal role in this rescue, and this is part of it."

"I...I don't cast spells," he stammered, his body as shaky as his speech.

"Okay, we do need one final element before you start. Do you have anything personal on you, something that matters to you?"

Luke's grin was slow, but it was true. "Pandora gave me this stone to ground me." The hematite was a dark stone with a slight silver shimmer. It had grounding and protective qualities. Pandora may not trust Tia, but she was blending into the family. In this case, it meant taking over Tia's role as magical guide.

The more she learned about the pipsqueak, the more she liked her. Scarlett wondered if she could get Luke to part with his treasure. "White magic is about give and take. You need to give something special to you in return for the help you are seeking."

He looked at the stone and was quiet for a while. She didn't rush him. He probably hadn't been given anything of value in a long time. Friendship and caring were in short supply. He may not be a child, but his needs were the same as any foster child: love, acceptance, and belonging. "Okay." He tried to hand it to her.

"Nope, not for me. You'll be adding it to the cauldron." She called a piece of paper from the arts and crafts table and imbued it will the spell, which took the form of swirling script written by an unseen pen. "First spell?"

"I've never." It was a rocky start but he finished confidently. "Yes, it is."

"Wicked." She handed him the spell. "Read through it a few times, and when you are ready, focus your intentions and cast the spell."

The first time he read through it, his shoulders were hunched as if weighed down by the responsibility. His posture straightened more with each pass. "I'm ready."

Scarlett smiled at him. "Yes. Yes you are." Luke reacted the way Jet and Onyx did when praised by her. She liked his aura and his growing inner strength.

I now ask the favor of having this spell removed. I understand to cancel a spell means giving up something of my own to show my spirit is true and my intentions are good. I give my protection stone. I cast the spell into the winds and render the spell dormant. No harm may come from the breaking of this spell. No further power shall it have. This is my will, so mote it be.

The cauldron accepted the gift and drew the positive intentions deep into the elixir. Scarlett removed the stopper from a small heart-shaped bottle. Its resemblance to a child's play perfume bottle was intentional. It may have looked like plastic, but it was something much heartier. The vessel was forged with a deep protection spell. Even Father would mistake it for a toy to go along with the set he had bought Magnolia. Scarlett called the elixir into the bottle and closed it. "Excellent work Luke." She put the bottle in the pouch attached to her leather belt. "You ready for the fun part?"

His eyebrows nearly met his hairline. Luke's confusion was priceless. "Fun is not a word I would use to describe this process."

"The magical residue in the cauldron has to be purged, completely obliterated."

"Just in case someone wants to cast a counterspell?"

Scarlett grinned. "No, but good thinking. This isn't the kind of spell that has a counter. It's just best not to leave any remnants behind." She didn't want to get into the details of what she added to the potion and the ramifications for breaking the curse. She surrounded the cauldron in a cloud of swirling purple and black smoke. The cast iron started to smolder. She mentally lifted the vessel then set the smoke on fire. The metal poured like molten lava toward her hands. Luke lunged her way to protect her from the lava, bless his heart. "I'm fine. Fire witch remember?"

"Oh, yeah. Right." His embarrassment turned to wonder as Scarlett transformed the lava into pumice rock. She crushed the black stone then inhaled the ashes. Scarlett grinned. She loved *recycling*.

Scarlett caught Luke before he hit the deck. She didn't blame him for fainting. Fire magic could be creepy as fuck. She picked him up as if he was a rag doll and tucked him into bed.

"Mama always told me to clean up my toys after I play."

Chapter Twenty-two

For the first time since the mirror incident, the kitchen felt like family. Angel had managed to make Pandora laugh hard enough to shoot milk through her nose, which of course made Kayla choke on her own saliva as she laughed and coughed her ass off.

Tia was at the head of the table enjoying the conversations, yet remaining quiet. She was putting on a brave face, but Tia's spirit was broken. She hadn't just lost her daughter, she'd lost her place in this household. Pandora and Kayla kidded with Sophia and gave Beau a case of the giggles. The room was warm, but Tia looked empty.

Winter poured hot water onto a bag of chamomile tea, and added a dollop of honey before resting the mug in front of her best friend. Tia looked up gratefully, and gave Winter a weak smile.

Scarlett slid into the free chair between Tia and Kayla. Even though Kayla was not engaging Scarlett in conversation, she felt friendly energy from the fifteen-year-old. They were the only ones at the table that had led truly dark lives. Kayla had been ping-ponged from foster home to group home and back again. She wasn't a troublemaker, but was often a target, especially once her powers had quickened. They sent her to juvie for arson after she set her closet on fire. Scarlett was sure that her firepower came as a shock to Kayla. She probably had accidentally conjured a fireball and had no idea what to do with it.

There were a lot of things that didn't make it into the file she had developed on Kayla, things that she read between the lines. The hardness in Kayla's eyes didn't start with Tia's dramatic slap. She had been abused, bullied, and at times, homeless. The streets were often safer than the homes foster children found themselves in. Scarlett was only three years older than Kayla, but her own childhood ended much earlier than Kayla's had. Her deadly training in mixed martial arts and dark magic started the moment her powers quickened. She made her first contract kill on the cusp of her teen years. At eighteen, she had a murderous decade under her belt.

Kayla was quite luminous when she smiled. Scarlett was admiring the blue eyes normally hidden behind Kayla's jagged black bangs and the smattering of freckles on her cheeks.

Scarlett smelled the ozone that she associated with Lilith.

Scarlett engaged Beau in some shenanigans, completely ignoring the livid teenager in the doorway. Kayla was too wrapped up in conversation to sense the scene that was about to unfold.

Lilith's blue hair was down and had white and gray streaks that ended in black tips. Her red lips were luscious and glossed. Scarlett wondered how people with lip piercings managed to put lipstick on without leaving a smudge on their jewelry.

Lilith would have made a metal detector go nuts. She had various metal loops and silver cuffs along the edges of both ears, a piercing through the cartilage at the bridge of her nose, and studs that gave her manmade dimples. Her thigh-high leather boots had mean looking buckles from top to bottom, which matched the embellishments on her black leather corset. She managed to make a red tartan miniskirt look badass. But the best part was her eyes, the electric blue swirling in her irises spoke of the fireworks that were yet to come.

Always one to tug a tiger's tail, Scarlett baited the punk rock girl. "Why don't you stop looking at the window display and come in the store? I think there's a sale on power trips."

All conversation stopped. Scarlett was the only one poised to enjoy the show. The first act was not what she expected, but was utterly predictable considering the level of Lilith's insecurity. The teen rounded the table, then kissed Kayla lightly on the mouth—it was a possessive move.

Kayla wasn't having it. "What's next Lilith? You gonna put your scent on me like a territorial cat? You don't own me and I don't care if she's sitting in your chair."

Boom! Now that was truly unexpected. Scarlett apparently had missed a lot in the week that she was gone. Kayla was out of her funk and on the defensive. This was a good sign for future missions, but a bad sign for the chemistry in the house.

Angel wasn't looking so angelic. She was angry. "Ripping each other's hearts to shreds won't bring Magnolia home any faster. Darkness may have touched your fingertips, but your choices are welcoming it into your blood."

Winter raised her eyebrows, probably surprised to see this amount of steel coming from sweet Angel.

"Scarlett brought this on, this is her doing. Get

rid of the Wicked White Witch and everything will go back to how it is supposed to be," Lilith countered. She looked ready to grab Scarlett by the scruff and toss her out on her ass.

Scarlett stood and pulled out the chair in a show of chivalry that would have made her own blood boil. "Have a seat. I'll be on my way." She wasn't storming off or mad at all. She knew that giving Lilith what she wanted would stir the shit pot even more.

Angel called out to her before she got far. "If you are done with the theatrics, we have business to attend to."

Scarlett's grin was cocky as hell. "As you wish."

Angel stood and her aura expanded. She had the presence of someone twice her size. "There is a price for all magic. There are rules that must be followed. Tia, you were the most vulnerable to temptation. That is why Scarlett was mind riding and not you. Your outburst proved this point and shattered something far more important: everyone's trust."

Tia shrunk in on herself. She looked so lost, but she needed a kick in the ass. She had to stop putting everyone's life at risk.

Winter rose and rested her hands on Tia's slumped shoulders. "Angel, I know you are saying things that must be said, but don't forget the feelings of those you call out."

Angel ignored Winter's attempt at smoothing things over. "The slap may have been the most dramatic side effect of your brush with dark magic, but it was not the most dangerous one." The room grew brighter as Angel neared the most salient point. "You were told not to try to contact Magnolia. The mother in you ignored this warning, which may be understandable, but by doing so, you put lives at risk."

"I didn't mean to," Tia said.

"Actually, you did. You resented being told what to do by your younger siblings, Scarlett in particular. She may be eighteen but she deserves more respect. If Scarlett hadn't cut the connection you made, she could have been executed for treason. Giovani wouldn't think twice about killing young Jonah, and Magnolia would have been taken away from her pretty little cage and stuck in someplace darker, someplace you couldn't reach if you tried."

Sophia took her daughter's hand as she absorbed these blows.

"This was all because you didn't take Scarlett seriously. You are so used to making the rules and telling people what path they need to take that you resented being on the other end of responsibility."

"I—I—" Tia stammered. "I didn't think. I didn't mean to." Tia looked like a child desperate to escape punishment.

Kayla stood up. The chair scraped against the floor as she faced off with Tia. "I can't believe this. Do you think you are so special that the rules don't apply to you?" She looked like she wanted to throw something. "Don't even try to squirm out of this. It's easy to do the right thing all the time when there is no temptation to break the rules. The second you were truly tested, you failed."

Tia wiped away her tears. Her eyes and nose looked raw. "I was being selfish. But Magnolia's my baby, and she's with someone very dangerous."

Angel knelt in front of Tia and rested her hands on her knees. "You need to fight against this desire. Your intense, desperate attempts to contact Magnolia made a connection deep inside Giovani's fortress. He had Magnolia on one side and Scarlett's room was on the opposite one. He could have heard you, Tia."

Tia was trembling. "I had no idea. I'm so very sorry."

Angel stood and leaned against the counter, to give Tia space to really hear what Angel was telling her. "I know you didn't know and that your inner mama bear was calling the shots. You've made mistakes. We all make mistakes. This is your chance Tia, to resist temptation and listen to those who have your best interests at heart. Beau and Scarlett may be young, but they are smart, thoughtful, and very powerful."

"Sure, stroke her ego. We'll never get her big head through the front door now," Sophia teased, tweaking Scarlett's nose playfully then making a face. Restrained giggles turned into full-on belly laughs. Tia was doing a cross between her ugly cry and rolling-on-the-floor laughing.

"The temptations coming your way are going to be increasingly hard to resist, but I believe in you, just as you believe in us." Angel smoothed her hands from the crown of Tia's head down the sides of her unruly curly hair.

"Help me Obi Wan, you're my only hope." Beau's Princess Leia was spot on.

Scarlett completely lost it. "Stop, stop. You're gonna make me pee."

Chapter Twenty-three

Darkness came early in late fall. She drove away from Tia's house with her windows rolled down. The air was filled with the sweet smell of wood burning fireplaces and a slight tang of apples. Scarlett liked driving along the apple orchard toward the abandoned farmhouse that she used to cross between worlds. The moments she spent in the void were quiet and peaceful.

The hearty tires on her Escalade absorbed most of the bounce as she touched down on the other side. She was relieved to get out of that kitchen. The heartbreak and regret was cloying, and she was looking forward to a long shower at home. Her cousins were sacked out on sectional couch. She wondered what they were escaping from. They were usually upbeat after an execution.

Her tired state didn't burn off her caution. She set her wards and locked down her space with newly designed passcodes. The randomizer she employed helped her avoid falling into predictability. The bathroom was soon filled with the scent of lilacs. It's what Sophia's home had smelled like before she left Giovani.

Sophia admitted that she hated the fragrance now because of the bad memories associated with her final days in the Dark Realm. Scarlett was surprised that Sophia lasted as long as she had. The gardens missed her more than Giovani, and he had truly loved her. Sophia wasn't an incubator like Ophelia or a hot lay like her mother Vivian.

Scarlett sat heavily on the bench attached to the shower wall. The humid floral air cleansed her mental cache and melted away the stress. Being on the light side was exhausting, and she was happy to leave the group to "process" their feelings. Scarlett hoped Tia's come-to-Jesus meeting was successful.

Her hair was damp enough to massage hot oil into. It took some time to attend to her voluminous locks, but she enjoyed the methodical indulgence. It was a form of meditation. She stood and activated the various jets, then bent forward until her head was pressed against the slick tiles. Water rushed down her back, soaking her hair completely. She had to be the only fire witch who thrived on water therapy.

Scarlett had contacted various informants to see if her father was checking up on her. Maxim said he wasn't playing peek-a-boo on the other side. She knew Father was reluctant to invade Sophia's space, as seeing her still hurt him. It was quite a blow to find out his former wife had a lesbian life partner. His reluctance worked in her favor. It probably was the reason why Rayne's *brilliant* plans went unnoticed for so long.

Scarlett changed the steam fragrance to coconut and honey. Her lovers often made comments how edible she always smelled. She didn't mind the bite marks—they made her feel alive.

Fans sucked the excess moisture from the air as she wrapped her head in a towel and shrugged into her soft cotton robe. Father said she wouldn't need her classy duds, so she was free to dress how she liked. He had some work for her to do. Scarlett hoped for something challenging and emotion free. Her clothing suitcase was heftier this time around since she didn't trust anyone with her laundry and wanted to get in some good workouts. Scarlett even packed some dressy clothes and a selection of wigs just in case her job assignments required femme drag.

The boys were snoring like buzz saws when she was ready to leave. She paused in the doorway, looking down on their sweet noisy forms. Their white skin and relaxed facial expressions made them look like angels. There was no irony in the observation. Lucifer had been an angel at one time, too.

She used a portal to shorten the drive to Giovani's castle. Scarlett giggled when the surveillance safe door was open. Her father had left a single rose resting inside the empty space. Finding the newly hidden devices was like an Easter egg hunt for spies. She was humming about Peter Cottontail as she set the new *crossword puzzle*. Scarlett let her mind wander as she unpacked—bunnies, mazes, flower bushes, and tea parties swirled around thoughts. "I wonder if Magnolia will like playing Alice."

Chapter Twenty-four

Scarlett was halfway to the gym when she encountered her father. "Want to spar?" she asked. She really loved sparring with her father. He was the only one who could whoop her ass in a fair fight. It had been a while since she needed to give it all she had.

"I'd like that."

Scarlett brightened. When her father didn't follow her, she turned around. "Not coming, or are we going to have some cloak and dagger fun?" She was warming up to the idea.

Giovani's smile reached his eyes. "Perhaps we can do so before you depart. Unfortunately I have a job that requires your immediate attention."

The professional side of her mind engaged, casting aside their familial connection in favor of cold calculation. "I packed for a wide range of possibilities. How may I be of service?"

He waved her to follow him through the catacomb of passageways until they entered his private office. The room smelled like leather and spice, and the furnishings were understated, just like his throne room. There was a large table he used to review maps and plot strategies old-school style. He also had a bank of huge flat screen televisions hooked up to a variety of equipment, while other devices accessed information wirelessly. She was impressed by the seamless blend of old and new.

He moved a family photo to the side, revealing a wide, shallow safe that was used for blueprints and large maps. There was a strange shimmer to the sheaves of paper he removed from the alcove. Scarlett's heart stopped when he spread out the paintings and sketches done in Magnolia's hand. They weren't museum quality works of art, but they far exceeded the ability of school children three times Magnolia's age.

They were a series of portraits of everyone in Tia's home. Giovani unconsciously traced the curve of Sophia's cheek. His love had never wavered. No one compared to Sophia.

She shoved down her fear as she flipped the large pages torn from the child's easel. Each page was a dry gunshot in this game of Russian roulette. She stilled as she flipped the last page. It was of the kitchen, tween Magnolia baking apple pie with Tia. The relief Scarlett felt made her lightheaded, but she gave no outward appearance of how hair-raising those moments had been. "She's really good. Would you like me to vet art instructors to continue her studies?" She was often asked to screen employees. Scarlett had an uncanny ability to spot assassins, opportunists, and spies. *Takes one to know one.*

Giovani leaned against the table, rustling the edges of the paintings that littered the wooden surface. "That's a fantastic idea, it hadn't occurred to me." He stared at her for a while, as if taking her measure. "Magnolia hasn't displayed the ability to conjure things with her artwork, which is a relief. We want her to use her adult voice, so she can quicken again, but these paintings could lead to a security breach."

She finally caught on. He was worried that Magnolia would forge a connection with her family and lead them to her doorstep. "They aren't powerful enough to breach your defenses Father. Beau and Tia are hopeless when it comes to dark magic. Their blood might grant them access to some places, but they're not savvy enough to find their way to her nursery. Better demons have tried and failed to reach your bedchamber."

"I agree with you. I'm not worried about the good witches snatching her up. Magnolia is the real problem." Giovani ran his hand through his wavy black hair, a more controlled sign of distress than Tia's frantic hair tugging. "She may be able to spring her own cell and get home without assistance. She casts powerful spells without even thinking."

Scarlett was so busy blocking Tia's attempts that she had forgotten Magnolia was powerful and stubborn enough to forge her own connection. "This probably won't go over well, but should you prevent her from painting or sketching?"

"She's as manageable as you were as a child, so no. She'd just start drawing on the walls. I need a more powerful solution. One that you may find beneath you." He crossed his arms over his chest. His ominous demeanor had been known to reduce full-grown men to piddling idiots. She didn't have that problem. "I need you to watch over Magnolia."

Scarlett would need to weigh out the pros and cons of being in such a key position. She would have to lean harder on Jonah, giving him a great deal more responsibility. He was ready, but she didn't like the idea of being penned in. "Magnolia's safety is a priority, and I would be happy to do security detail, but not full-time. I have other responsibilities."

He nodded, happy with her lack of resistance.

"There is another, equally pressing mission that I need you to take the lead on."

Scarlett had not a fucking clue as to what could be more urgent than Magnolia's care. The heat and anger her father was broadcasting was enough to melt the decorative candles in the antique sconces around the room. Rage this maddening was reserved for blood relatives. Maybe he had caught her in the act and was testing her reactions to the images and protection detail.

"Someone has freed Rayne. I executed the guilty party and his entire family. That's why Jet and Onyx are passed out in your den. It was a large family." He gestured to the artwork, which gathered itself and flew into the safe. The tumblers in the safe lock snapped closed with a satisfying click. Father was sentimental over safes and battlements from his younger years. His magic secured the safes; the locks were merely quaint accessories. "Does Rayne still trust you?"

Scarlett strode toward the narrow window that was designed for archers' arrows. Very little light came through, but there was plenty of space for the archers and their bows. "I'm not quite sure. Even if he doesn't, Rayne is easily manipulated and naive. His ego overpowers his common sense. He's probably still pouting over Belladonna."

Giovani shook his head. "The only way he could bed her would be via necrophilia, but her body is too ruined for sport."

"Even if her corpse was pristine, he wouldn't have a shot. She'd figure out how to snub him, even in death," Scarlett said with a sardonic smile.

Giovani's chuckle was throaty and bone-chilling at the same time. "He's always been a failure, a truly pathetic boy. I should have killed him when he was a squalling pup."

Scarlett brushed her hand down the coarse surface of the archers' window. "You would have had to have been a fish to get near him."

Giovani strode to his desk and removed a pouch. The deep clinking sound came from gold coins, another nod to the past he wished he could return to. He handed her the leather pouch that had a set of keys in addition the hefty bag of gold coins. She used the leather straps to secure the pouch around her trim waist. "Which mission first?"

Giovani escorted her to the door. "I'll leave that to your judgment. See how close Magnolia is to forging a connection. If it's to communicate, Rayne's capture is a priority. If you think Magnolia can create a portal she can use to return to home, stay with her."

"If it's the latter, shall I lock her in the tower?" Scarlett didn't want to do this, but she'd rather spring her niece from the tower than the room right next to her father. Either way, Magnolia's days in the castle were numbered.

Giovani chuckled. "She might like that. Adriana says *Rapunzel* is her favorite story."

"There's some irony in that. Don't worry, Father. She won't come to harm on my watch." The risk involved in her new position gave her an adrenaline rush.

"Murder Rayne if you have to."

The order was a buzzkill. "It would be my final act of kindness." Rayne would wish he were dead long before Father would allow him such mercy.

"You always had a soft spot for him." Giovani looked her square in the eye. "I will expect proof." He handed her two boxes; one was small enough to fit in her pouch and the other was the size of her motorcycle helmet. "You may eat his soul, but bring his powers to me. I will feed his creampuff of skull to Maxim's hounds."

"Brains, part of a balanced breakfast."

Chapter Twenty-five

Scarlett sat heavily on her bed and contemplated her options. There really were two. The first was to kill her brother quickly and return with his head, soul, and magic in boxes. The latter would be in the form of orbs. She wouldn't eat her brother's soul. She was not a monster. The second option was to return him to the castle and let Father take care of him. Either way, her brother's blood would be on her hands.

She picked up the larger box, which was deceptively simple. Matte black, no adornments, locks, or buckles. She opened the lid and unhinged the sides so it was completely flat. It would fold down into a shape that she could easily fit in her kill bag. Scarlett packed her sleeping bag, tent, rations, and various items she would need for the hunt. She probably wouldn't know if she would actually go through with it until the kill moment presented itself.

A child's scream raised the hair on Scarlett's arms. She rushed through the back corridor and thrust open the door to Magnolia's nursery. What she saw made her nauseous. She picked up a squalling Magnolia, then escaped the room. She didn't know if the murderer lingered.

"Shhhh shhhh shhhh, darlin'. I got you." Scarlett eased Magnolia's fright with a sleeping spell. The child sagged against her as she navigated the twists and turns that would lead to the tower. She heard footfalls and heavy breathing coming from behind her.

She was about to blaze the pursuer into oblivion, when Jonah called out to her. "It's me. I had to gather a few things before I could follow." The boy was wheezing, he was not built for the speed of her escape.

"Jonah, I'll let you know once I have settled. Go another way. Gather supplies. Oh fuck, my pouch." The anti-aging potion was in the pouch she left in her room.

"Got it." He tossed it to her before the path forked, and she went left while he went right. Scarlett paused, created a shimmering oval and walked through it into the tower room. No staircases were connected to the tower and the walls could not be scaled. This stronghold could not be ambushed.

Now that they were safe, Scarlett sat down on the chest at the foot of a four-poster bed. The canopy was as dreamy as the mountain of pillows on the mattress. Stuffed animals and lifelike dolls were nestled in the thick comforter. There was an arts and crafts area with tons of supplies, and a lot of other things to entertain the now slumbering child. Her father had given much thought to designing Magnolia's room.

As her heart rate returned to normal, she allowed herself to process the gory scene in Magnolia's nursery. Adriana was suspended from the ceiling, scorched from head to toe. Her neck was bent at an unnatural angle. The next image took her breath away. Magnolia's bed was soaked with water and the rug beneath it was completely saturated. Rayne had been thrown up against the canopy with such force that his head and broken left arm had punched through the fabric. His chest had a gaping hole where his heart had been. The wound was created by a high velocity fireball.

Scarlett didn't have to ride Magnolia's mind to piece together what had happened. Adriana had let Rayne into Magnolia's room with the intent to murder the toddler. She took a deep breath, followed by another.

Magnolia was fast asleep but she was shivering violently. Her nightgown was soaked completely with lurid splashes of blood and scorched human remains. No child should ever have to see this. She held Magnolia close to her body as she located a new nightgown and underwear in the dresser next to the armoire. The bathroom was large but child friendly. There were two toilets—a small one for Magnolia and a regular sized one for adult guests. She rested the clothing on the sink then started a bath in the claw-foot tub. She tipped some sweet smelling bubble soap into the swirling water while keeping Magnolia cradled in her arms.

Scarlett sat down on the tiles beside the bathtub and carefully removed Magnolia's soiled clothing. She tugged a fluffy white towel from the nearby rack and folded it into a temporary bed. The room was filling with the scent of bubblegum. Magnolia smiled in her sleep.

Scarlett chuckled when she saw a set of her own clothing beneath the standing sink. That was a Jonah touch if she ever saw one. Scarlett locked the bathroom door and set a warding so no one could barge in on them. She felt gross, but only indulged in a fresh dry set of clothing after she scrubbed herself clean with a hand towel. The dirty clothes went into the trash, which thankfully had a lid to hold in the stench. She would have just incinerated them, but there had been enough fire for one night.

The bathwater was only six inches deep, and the

bubbles were even thicker. She washed the child. Once all the yucky stuff was off of her, Scarlett pulled the drain plug. When Scarlett was certain the signs of the attack had gone down the drain, she let the little one wake up as she refilled the tub.

"Oooh, I loves bubbles." She splashed around. Maybe Magnolia thought what happened had been a dream. If so, Scarlett planned to keep it that way. "Oooooh oh oh oh youz mama's sissy! I know I saw you before." Magnolia scooped up a big fluff of bubbles and blew them at Scarlett.

"That tickles my nose! Silly willy." Scarlett amused Magnolia by calling the bath toys from the basket under the sink and plunking them into the soapy water. "You're a lot like me. I didn't think there were other firestarters who loved water so much."

Magnolia smiled, then turned her slippery body on her belly so she could blow bubbles of her own beneath the surface. She slithered until she was right side up and started to sing "Row, Row, Row Your Boat."

Scarlett joined her. She needed this nourishing moment. There would be a lot of explaining to do once Magnolia was settled.

"Why you have no colors?" Magnolia tugged on a loose lock of Scarlett's hair.

"This is the way I was made. Some people are born albinos."

"I gives you colors when we dwaw. You'll be purty as a wainbow." Magnolia rested her wet hands on Scarlett's cheeks and gave her a smacking kiss on the lips. "I love you, mama's sissy."

She didn't mind the tears slipping down her own cheeks. It was a release of stress, and the only sign of mourning she could afford for a long time. She actually liked that Magnolia didn't tell her to stop crying, and she seemed utterly okay with strong emotions. That had Tia written all over it. "And I love you, swirly girly."

Chapter Twenty-six

Jonah was facing three very serious fire witches: Scarlett, Giovani, and Pyron, Giovani's brother. Jonah didn't seem concerned and Scarlett wondered at that. All Jonah's life, he had been either ignored or bullied. His response in the past was to try and be as invisible as possible. This was not the best time to become defiant.

Giovani was not amused. "How did Adriana get access to Magnolia's room after hours?"

"I don't know. I didn't let her in."

Giovani leaned over the table in the interrogation room and got in Jonah's face. "So you let my ingrate of a son in and she was along for the ride?" The wooden surface smoldered as if a hot iron was branding Giovani's fingerprints onto the surface. "Where have you been hiding Rayne?"

"I didn't hide him." Jonah was unfazed by Giovani's mounting anger and Scarlett wanted to know why. It was as if he was being strengthened by an unseen force. At first, she had objected to his interrogation. Jonah was a child and had been extremely loyal in the past, but his absence during the attack was suspicious. Scarlett also didn't appreciate that he had been in her room while she was rescuing Magnolia, and that he knew her room well enough to grab the pouch with the potion.

Pyron was as tall and imposing as his brother, but where Giovani was dark and swarthy, he was light.

He was not albino like his sons, but his light blond hair and fair skin was a closer match to the pale-skinned warriors in the family.

Scarlett's uncle casually broke Jonah's pinky on his left hand. "I will break your fingers one at a time, and if that fails to loosen your lips, I'll cut them down, one joint at a time."

Jonah grimaced and looked less confident.

Pyron pinched Jonah's ring finger and was poised to snap it if he did not get the answers he was looking for. "Your duty was to protect the princess."

"She's not a princess, she's a bastard."

Giovani crushed Jonah's right wrist, and this time the boy did scream.

"Father." Scarlett turned to face Pyron. "Uncle. May I? I have a feeling that Jonah has grown too accustomed to physical pain."

Something glinted in Pyron's eyes before it winked out like a flame in a strong wind gust. "Of course."

"Jonah, I can tear the truth from your brain, but if it's locked down as tight as I think it is, the retrieval will lead to brain death." Scarlett didn't want to do that to Jonah. "The problem is that you keep so many secrets and now that your loyalty has been tarnished, you can't be trusted." She pressed her lips firmly in a line. She was frustrated, but knew she had to be smart if she was going to get what she wanted from this interrogation.

"Father, I'd like to take his magic away and lock up his mind before we put him in the dungeon." All the color drained from Jonah's face. Scarlett had guessed right; his mind and his powers were everything to Jonah. "That way he can tell no secrets and will not be able to escape on his own."

Pyron snapped the finger he had been holding. It

was a form of pouting. He had obviously been looking forward to some serious, prolonged torture. "I'd like to sweep his room and the place where he kept his things while caring for Magnolia."

Giovani obviously didn't trust his brother enough for this task. "I appreciate the offer, but I think Scarlett will be able to spot things we might miss. She knows Jonah better than we do. I'll keep you apprised of everything relevant."

Pyron deferred to his brother, as he always did. "As you wish. I will see what I can learn from my men."

Scarlett resented the emphasis on *men*, since many of those under Pyron's leadership were women.

Giovani clapped him on the shoulder. "Thank you, brother. You have so much to do in addition to this matter that I won't keep you any longer."

Pyron nodded to both, then winked at Scarlett. "By your leave."

Giovani turned back to the prisoner. "Jonah, I will give you one last opportunity to be honest with us. What role did you play in the attack?"

Jonah chose to keep his silence, which forced Scarlett to make his silence permanent. "Father, silence his power while I lock down his mind. I don't want him to get any wise ideas."

Giovani chuckled. "I've always enjoyed your sense of humor."

"So, we need to put the lad in a safe place and apparently we have a loyalty problem amongst our jailors. A lead casket would be fitting."

Jonah promptly swooned.

Scarlett giggled.

"Like I said." Giovani's smile was sincere and met his eyes. "I do enjoy your sense of humor."

Chapter Twenty-seven

"The next time you have a chase scene, have a heart and give me notice so I can heat up some popcorn." Maxim was using the magical version of Skype, his flawless face broadcast into the mirror of Scarlett's current bedroom. She liked her new digs, with less security necessary and no sneaky corridors. The latter was both a good and a bad thing.

"You're a pretty little dork, aren't ya? Damn those ditzy blondes, everything is must-see TV this, reality TV that." Maxim stuck out his tongue, he was *so* mature. "Sometimes Seer, you are a master of understatement. I knew Magnolia was crazy powerful, but what I didn't know was that she was more capable of taking care of herself than half of Father's demon army."

Maxim sobered immediately. "I get how Rayne became a maimed puppet, but how on earth did she manage to hang Adriana, snap her neck, and roast her like a marshmallow in the seconds between her scream and your arrival?"

"She's still a little hazy on the details, but my guess is that her old soul took over. Magnolia's soul has had eons of military experience, and her counterattack was like muscle memory on steroids."

"The question of the century is, why has she not aged to, I don't know...a senior citizen after that particular outburst?"

Scarlett had watched Magnolia for signs of premature aging for what was left of that crazy night, but she remained the sweet chubby cherub that she had rescued from the nursery. "I have no idea. It has to be related to being in the Dark Realm. I did, however, give her the potion to avoid a delayed reaction." Magnolia had told her that the next time Scarlett made her drink something yucky to remember to use a spoonful of sugar like Mary Poppins did. Scarlett had laughed until she cried.

"No side effects at all? She didn't go all retrograde on you?"

Scarlett wasn't exactly sure how the curse worked, only that it didn't seem to affect Magnolia in the Dark Realm. There was definitely more to it, but unless she interrogated Lykos, she was unlikely to unravel all the elements behind the spell. "Could you imagine me returning a newborn Magnolia to Tia? That would go over well. If there is any moment a mom wants to return to, it's all-night feedings and so little sleep that parents become the walking dead for months."

"Oooh, she could blame you for her first gray hairs!" Maxim touched his perfect blond hairdo. "I'd never forgive you."

"There was one side effect." Scarlett's heart was heavy. "The potion brought back some of Magnolia's memories from Rayne's attack." Scarlett had hoped Magnolia would continue to think of that the wretched night as bad dream. "At least Magnolia had a few nights of freedom before the gruesome memories resurfaced. She seemed oddly at peace with what had happened."

"I'm sure Tia would love to hear that." Maxim rolled his gorgeous blue eyes and then crossed them. "By the way, Tia's been a bit berserk since it happened."

Scarlett bit her lip. Her sister had become a loose cannon and a nuisance. She had better things to do than police Tia's behavior. "What's she done now?"

"She's acting like the teenagers she is supposed to be guiding and taking care of." Scarlett wanted to bang her head against the wall. The bullshit Tia was pulling was no longer putting lives at risk, but her foster children were another matter altogether. "How long until Kayla and Pandora fly the coop?"

Maxim rubbed his face. "Soon, very soon."

"Is that your witchy opinion?" Scarlett's bun didn't feel right. It was pulled too tight on the left and there was an unruly loop that was sticking out. She took it down, then tugged it into a high ponytail. She wished the mirror was still reflective so she could check if her hair was smooth to her scalp.

"You look marvelous. As for the girls, they're packing. I'll give you the instant replay in a second. What are we going to do about them? Someone is on the loose, and I'm not altogether convinced this plot was Rayne's idea. It's far too sophisticated. Morgana is not that inept at setting wards and casting protection spells. Rayne shouldn't have been able to get in and Adriana doesn't have late-night access."

Scarlett paced as she thought things through. Maxim was right. Rayne was Giovani's lesser son. Father could have forgiven his magical affinity if he was a master practitioner, but Rayne was far from it.

She pulled a seven-inch blade from a sheath attached to her hip. She manipulated it like her mother often did. Deadly instruments helped her focus. "Tia said something unusual about their enemy. She called the ominous presence *The Darkness*. Rayne is a bully, not a mastermind. Belladonna and Xavier together could have wreaked havoc, but they didn't exactly have the ability to create such a powerful dark presence."

Maxim suddenly looked on high alert. "As much as I'm enjoying this game of Clue, we have a problem. Kayla and Pandora, in their infinite wisdom, escaped while the house slept."

"Oh for fuck's sake! They're thinking like street kids, not like the powerful witches they are. Their combined abilities would be a beacon for anyone seeking an easy mark." Scarlett reached into her back pocket and texted the most reliable hunter she knew and gave her the short version.

"Which direction are they headed?" Scarlett asked Maxim, then texted the coordinates to the hunter. Scarlett's phone rang before she even got to click send. "Mother, normally I would take care of this myself, but I need to stay with Magnolia. Plus, you are the only one I trust who also is immune to fire."

"Oh this should be fun." She could sense Vivian's excitement. Her mother's work was often monotonous and predictable. "I know Kayla's a firestarter, but does Pandora has any offensive abilities?"

Scarlett liked how practical her mother was. "Maxim?" Scarlett asked the mirror.

"Pandora is a necromancer. She's only at the I-see-dead-people stage. She can't enlist ghosts to help her."

"Ya hear that, Mom?"

"Loud and clear. Where shall I take the runaways?" Scarlett could hear a rustle of fabric and a few clinks, followed by the sound of a thick zipper closing.

"I don't trust them in my house without supervision." Pandora had a knack for theft and lock picking. She could get into trouble of the deadly variety.

"Maxim?"

Maxim's grin was reserved, but he was more excited than he was letting on. He may have been a hermit, but he loved to entertain. "Shall I let them find their own way in, you know, keep things lively?"

Like Scarlett, Maxim also loved to collect booby traps and various animal snares. "Pandora may be up for it, but we need both on our side. Trust is in short supply."

"Vivian darling, you'll join me for breakfast? I have an errant soul or two ripe for consumption."

Scarlett giggled, But Maxim was dead serious.

"How could I say no to that?" Vivian asked. "I can't resist your many hosting wiles. I'll make this hunt short and sweet. Scarlett darling, I'll have to bind and blindfold them, but I promise they won't be injured." Scarlett heard her mother spritz cologne. She was a sentimental like Father. Vivian collected antique perfume bottles with tasseled atomizers that needed to be squeezed to release fragrance.

Scarlett's mother may be unconventional, but she trusted her. "Do what you have to do."

Vivian hung up without saying goodbye. She was polite like that.

Scarlett slipped her knife back into its sheath and gave Maxim her full attention. "Now that that's been taken care of, cue up the DVR recording of Tia's tantrum."

"Your wish is my command."

Chapter Twenty-eight

"Don't you dare tell me to calm down, Beau." Tia was rubbing a dish so hard it was bound to break her in hands. She tossed it into the clear water of the second sink. One dish after another was viciously cleaned.

"Tia," Beau whispered so only the two could hear. "Tia honey, Magnolia is fine. Scarlett said so, and I believe her. I'm not telling you to calm down for me, but you have an audience."

Beau dried each dish with careful hands, as if apologizing to them for Tia's rough treatment. He put them away, then started on the chaos of the island which was cluttered with debris from breakfast.

Kayla and Pandora were drawing and giggling. So far, Kayla had conjured a baby dragon to play with Pandora's mini unicorn. Lilith was pouting so loud that Kayla glitter bombed her.

Lilith stood and growled. "Seriously. I'll never get the glitter out of this outfit." She dusted off some of the sparkling confetti, but it was hopeless. The glitter embedded itself in Lilith's suede and velvet corset. Bits clung to the folds of her black Victorian skirt. "Grow up, Kayla."

Kayla's smile vanished. "Growing up doesn't seem to be working in this household, and I will do whatever I damn well please. You don't own me." Kayla stood up and held a jar filled with a filthy combination of watercolor and acrylic paint water. "You need to back off. I didn't ask you to sit down with us, and I don't want you anywhere near us."

"You wouldn't dare." The threat in Lilith's voice was ominous.

Kayla swirled the dirty water. "What makes you so sure?"

The sound of shattering glass made Kayla drop her weapon. The dirty water soaked the table, ruining their artwork.

"Stop it!" Tia shouted as she smashed the food-encrusted casserole dish on the center island. "I've had it with you too tearing each other's hearts apart. Kayla, if you don't want Lilith, tell her. Don't torture her with your friendship with Pandora."

"You've got nerve to tell anyone how to act in this house, Tia," Kayla jabbed. "You've been one temper tantrum after another. Act like a fucking adult for once. Come on, Pandora."

Tia swept her arm across the island splashing glass and perishables all over the hardwood floors. The destructive act made Kayla pause briefly, her disgust evident.

Scarlett cringed. She couldn't believe how ugly this situation was getting.

Winter ran into the kitchen from the back porch. The screen door clacked ominously, as if it knew what was about to happen. "Tia, that's quite enough. You apologize to them." Winter's fury was intense. "This is not how we treat each other. If you don't straighten out your act, I'm going to have to find a better placement for the girls."

The whole room seemed to be sucked of oxygen. Tia looked as if she was going to shatter like the shards she scattered across the floor.

"This is a haven for foster children who need a good home. A place that is safe, a sanctuary." Winter didn't need a hand to strike her best friend. "What example are you setting for Pandora? All she has ever seen here is your violence and temper. I know this was not how you were raised."

Beau flowed toward Winter like water trying to put out an inferno, but the damage was done. "Winter, she's been—"

"I'm done with excuses. These children matter just as much as Magnolia does. They need a mother, and if you can't be that, then you might as well pack their bags." Winter seemed to gather herself, calming a bit. "You need to sit down, and consider the way Scarlett has handled this matter. She has behaved with fairness and dignity, always keeping the best interests of those she loves at heart. That is who you used to be. I don't know how, but you better find that woman and be her again."

The mirror shimmered, leaving the chilling tableau behind. Maxim's expression was grim. "It's worse seeing the second time around."

"Holy fuck! I can't even..." Scarlett's mouth kept opening and closing as she started and dismissed several responses. "I'm a fucking assassin, a gun for hire."

"You've always been much more than that. Truly." Maxim looked her directly in the eyes. "You are respected because of who you are, not in spite of what you are."

"But...but...Tia..." Scarlett was at a loss, as if gravity had ceased to work and the world was flat. "I'm no role model."

Maxim crossed his arms and widened his stance. "On the Earthly Realm, usually not, but here you are."

"Come on." Her brain was rattling around in her head. The scene in the kitchen was far more distressing than the one she rescued Magnolia from.

"As much as I'd like to defend your honor and my point of view, we have a far more pressing issue." Maxim tapped the mirror from his side. "Tia. I'm afraid for her."

Scarlett nodded. Tia's world was punctured by the loss of her daughter, but what had taken place since Magnolia went missing was far more disturbing. Tia had lost her daughter, her identity and her place in this world. "I would go to her, but after what Winter said…"

"No shit, she'd probably commit *seppuku* right in front of you."

Seppuku was the response samurai warriors had to disgrace, ritually falling on their sword leading to death by disembowelment. Maxim wasn't being overly dramatic; the risk of suicide was real. "Then what? I can't stand by while she kills herself."

Maxim tugged his lip and frowned. "You have to give her something to live for."

"Magnolia's not enough?"

He shook his head sadly.

"The assassin has to give someone a reason to live. As if I didn't have enough irony in my diet."

Chapter Twenty-nine

Kayla felt nauseous. She may have seemed badass when she was mouthing off, but inside she was scared. Scared of the responsibility of caring for Pandora and scared of the changes in Tia.

She loved Tia and had grown to count on her in the months since she'd been placed there. This was the first home she had ever lived in where she didn't feel like a freak show, but more importantly, this was the first place she had lived where she didn't have to worry about getting beaten or abused. Kayla didn't think Tia would actually hurt them. She was just broken and all fucked up inside since Magnolia was taken. A part of Kayla was happy that Tia wasn't perfect all the time, but this wasn't about Kayla anymore. This was about Pandora, and she wouldn't let her down.

"Do you think she will notice that we've gone? Winter's smackdown has to have Tia on edge." Pandora was not as cagey as she was when she first showed up, but she was still very thin, and vulnerable emotionally. Pandora was both strong and fragile at the same time. Kayla might have been able to ride the situation out until Tia got her act together. She wasn't so sure about Pandora.

"I think she's too fucked up to notice. Winter was harsh, not that Tia didn't deserve what she got, but the look on her face as we left the room tore my heart out." Kayla had gotten used to expressing her emotions since she moved here. A few weeks of crazy couldn't undo the good Tia and her family had brought into Kayla's life. That's why leaving this way was so damned hard. "Tia may be acting out, but she's not evil. That doesn't matter, though. We can't stay."

The threat of a new placement was the biggest danger, and she knew for sure no home would take her *and* Pandora. Even if they did, their magical abilities would get them kicked out or worse. Kayla would not risk them being institutionalized. A nut house or juvie, they were two shades of the same hell. There was no way on earth she would expose Pandora to that kind of danger, especially since her life had been fairly easy up until this point.

"I'm all set. I never had much stuff to pack. I'm so little all my clothes fit in my book bag." Pandora actually looked excited, as if they were going on a great adventure, but Kayla knew better.

"Was the same for me until I got here. I wish you could have seen what it was like before all hell broke loose. This was a special place." Packing was a heartbreaking process. She'd have to leave behind the art supplies that Lilith had given her, and most of her clothes. The new ones Tia had bought her made the cut.

"That's what you keep sayin'. So where are we heading once we blow this Popsicle stand?"

Kayla had no fucking idea. "For now, there is bridge by a set of train tracks. We can go there to think. Who knows, Tia might come to her senses and act like a mom for once, and we can come back."

"She's worse than the alcoholic mother from my last placement. At least her brand of crazy was predictable."

The backpack Kayla nicked was Beau's, which he used when he wandered all over the world. It was in good shape and had some helpful things like a first aid kit and a flare. Kayla had to laugh at the latter; she was a human flare.

"You're not going nuts on me, are ya?" Pandora had adorable dimples and she was still pure of spirit. She had been an outsider, but suffered nothing worse than neglect. Kayla would do her best to protect Pandora from the darker things.

"Not yet, but you'll be the first to know." Kayla tucked in the snacks, water, and anything else that would be useful but not too heavy to carry. They'd have to share the sleeping bag, but as skinny as they both were that wouldn't be a problem. "You ready?"

Pandora's lovely brown eyes lit up and her smile crinkled her freckles. The kid was adorable. "Absolutely. Are we climbing out or using the front door?"

"Wait here a minute. I'll go check to see if anyone is up in the kitchen or the meditation space." The kitchen was no longer a shattered minefield, but a trip to the store to replace what had been broken was in order. She caressed the smooth surface of the island. Kayla ate her first real meal there. The fried chicken was out of this world, never mind Sophia's famous sweet tea. This place used to be a home. She hoped that it could be that again, but she just couldn't afford to wait around to find out.

The meditation space smelled sweet and earthy. Someone had been there earlier in the evening, but the incense had burned out. The ashes looked like gray caterpillars. She had so many memories associated with this space. She choked back a sob as a hazy memory of Angel's memorial resurfaced. The ache in her chest overpowered any lingering sentimentality. She knew that it wasn't possible, but she wished Angel could have stuck around after her visit.

She showed Pandora where to put her feet to avoid the creaky steps, which ended up being some fancy footwork, since this was an old house. Kayla kept her eyes forward as they walked out the door. They needed to get out before they were discovered. Kayla looked back at the old Victorian that had been her first real home since her grandmother died. She hoped this goodbye was temporary.

Kayla's heart calmed once they reached the train tracks. This was where she used to go when she needed a place to chill and have time alone. Kayla had really hoped Tia's home was lucky thirteen. For some reason this failed placement hurt more than all the other twelve combined. "The bridge is just around the bend. we can sleep there for the night."

Pandora fell fast asleep as soon as she snuggled into the sleeping bag, but Kayla was too on edge to join her. The bizarre sound of hoofbeats made her tense, like she was in some twisted version of the Three Billy Goats Gruff. Magnolia had loved that bedtime story, but Kayla always found it creepy.

Clip-clop, clip-clop, clip-clop.

In a swirl of darkness and fire, a demon swung from a rope into their hiding place. The woman who materialized from the smokescreen was a sinister version of Belladonna.

"I should skin you alive for comparing me to that vapid tart. I'm not sorry she is dead." The demon wore a black leather jumpsuit unzipped far enough to showcase a pirate-worthy white blouse. Lilith would so steal the thigh-high stiletto boots. "Ah yes, your paramour. Now she reminds me of myself when I was a girl. She is a born killer," the woman said with a smile. Kayla could tell that this was the ultimate compliment.

Pandora had woken and was ready to fight. There was this odd sound of shuffling from the darkness under the bridge and along the train tracks.

"Wonderful. She sees dead people and can call them to her." The demon sounded like calling the dead was on the same nuisance level as a tear in her nylons. It was fucking creepy to Kayla. Flames licked at her fingers, a sure sign of her agitation.

"As much as I would enjoy toying with the wee ghosties, there isn't time. I'm Vivian by the way. You know my daughter. Scarlett sent me to fetch you before you could get into any real trouble."

Kayla glanced around wildly, desperate to make an escape. *This is all my fuckin' fault and Pandora is going to pay the price.* "Please, tell Scarlett you couldn't find us. We don't want any trouble."

Vivian's laughter was musical and dark. A few of the looming ghosts stopped to admire her. "You *are* trouble Kayla, and so is the little one." Vivian threw a force field net like the one Scarlett used to trap a pissed off Lilith in the attic. The demon spoke in a language Kayla couldn't understand, and the result chilled her. Her hands and ankles were bound, and a silk scarf slithered across her face on its way to being tied behind her head. She was now effectively immobile and blind. "Don't worry Kayla fair. Maxim will surely welcome you in a style you might want to become accustomed to. Nighty-night."

Darkness swamped Kayla's mind.

Chapter Thirty

Even though Magnolia was on the other side of the meeting room door, Scarlett felt anxious about not having her in sight. Jet was playing with her. She had never seen his soft side, but Magnolia was kinda irresistible. She wondered if her cousin was currently getting "colors" from the toddler.

"Daughter, you can feel her fire and we've reduced full access to you and me. The only permitted guests are family. Jonah may have been pliable; Jet and Onyx are not."

Scarlett thought it was interesting that Father had excluded Pyron from the list of permitted guests. This was obviously an inside job and her uncle was the weakest link in the line now that Rayne was dead. "I agree on that front. My cousins have about as much power as they desire at the moment."

Giovani smiled, as he always did when thinking of his favorite executioners. "Not for lack of ambition."

"That's something many people in the kingdom miss." Jet and Onyx loved power, but their thirst for freedom was stronger. Ascending to the throne was incompatible with coming and going as they pleased. "The lack of understanding extends to mother and I. Neither of us wants to be queen."

Giovani leaned back against the heavy oak table. It was a six-inch slice from the heart of a tree, with legs sturdy enough for rough handling. It was a throwback to Giovani's younger years. He liked older things around him when matters grew truly serious. "That is why I trust you the way I do."

Scarlett felt bad that she kept so much from her father, especially when he was being affectionate. She loved him, but couldn't escape her true nature. "I value your approval, though I doubt I am truly trustworthy."

Giovani's laugh was deep and throaty.

Even Magnolia heard him. "No-no iz laughin'. I didn't know No-no has laughin' in him." Scarlett got a kick out of Magnolia's language. She might have been using baby talk, but Magnolia was wiser than she appeared. It was always best to be underestimated by an enemy, and that kind of lapse in judgment had made many of her assignments easy kills.

"You are a demon and my child, so of course you have secrets from me. I allow them to flourish. True mysteries and secrets are in short supply for a man of my age." Giovani was immortal and ancient, but he looked like a swarthy man in the prime of his life. He was tall, powerfully built, with tan skin and eyes as blue as the Mediterranean. Eyes that turned liquid silver when he was angry. "The most salient point, when it comes to family and murderous plots, is that you have no desire to see me dead."

Scarlett pulled out her hunting knife, which had a wicked blade, strong enough to puncture even Vivian's skin. "Are you that sure?" Faster than the eye could see, she threw the knife so close to her father that the fabric of his pants rippled in the slight breeze it kicked up.

"Like I said." Giovani yanked at the hilt of the deeply embedded knife, twirled it like a baton, then threw it at his daughter's head. She caught it with the flats of her hands. The tip dimpled the skin on her forehead. "I enjoy your sense of humor."

Scarlett returned the blade to its scabbard. "When this is all over, I want to spar. You long for mystery as much as I crave a challenge."

The sound of Jet singing a nursery rhyme with Magnolia made Scarlett sputter with laughter. "I hope you have a camera rolling. He's bound to be snookered into a tea party."

Giovani laughed again.

"No-no iz laughin'! Why not he come and play Milkman?"

"Milkman?" Giovani asked. "Is milkman a game? I've never heard of it."

Scarlett thought a moment then chuckled. "That must be the Dark Prince's new nickname."

Giovani smiled as if he could see the two at play. "Why don't we keep the humor going and summon Arcana and her consort…"

"Silvia, Medusa's bastard child." The jibe was a familiar one. Silvia's main affinities were for water and animals, reptiles in particular. Medusa was a mythological creature, and unlike the gorgon, Silvia was quite beautiful. Her snakelike hair was charming. Scarlett smirked at her own pun.

"Yes, Silvia and Cane. Just enough power to be dangerous, but not enough to rule."

"Sometimes those are the most troubling demons." The hunger for a power that was just out of reach, yet never attainable, would make any demon bitter. Arcana had every power in the book but fire. Without fire, powerful transcendent fire, she could never rule in this kingdom. "I can't see them grooming Jonah. Cane hates perceived weakness. She would squash him like a cockroach. Your sister doesn't exactly play well with others."

Giovani pressed his hand to the door. He truly loved those on the other side. "Magnolia is a prize she might be willing to compromise for."

"She would still need someone with fire power to help her."

This didn't give her father much comfort. An army of lessor fire witches could combine forces. "The big question is, what demon is willing to share their flame?"

"I have a feeling that some will share their flame unwillingly," Scarlett said. It was possible to consume the powers of murdered demons. "We need to ask Mother to be on the lookout for wasted fire witches."

"They would need to pile them up like cords of wood to defeat me." Giovani stared at the wall shared with the nursery. "If they ate Magnolia's soul, there would be no safe shadow in either realm."

Chapter Thirty-one

"On that cheerful note, let's have some fun shall we. Which one first?" Scarlett asked in a sing-song voice. Both women would put on a show. She eyed their surroundings, looking for channels to wick away the sheets of water that always accompanied Silvia's arrival. If the two lovers were somewhere together, a full on deluge was possible. "Both pose a flood risk, and I really like my new digs."

"Iz gives you colors Milkman, purty colors. Blue and purple and green and…"

"Ha-ha, can I have a little peek before we bring on the ladies?" Scarlett wanted a front row seat. "On second thought, I don't want any 'colors.'"

"Silvia first. It would give my sister a nice little scare for her lovey to go missing."

"You are truly evil!" And Scarlett loved it. Being bad could feel really good sometimes.

Giovani's smile was incandescent. "Flattery will get you everywhere. As for April showers, this should take care of the water without making us vulnerable." Even the smallest holes in a tower could give a demon access. "I have to say this was an ingenious invention. Kali deserves a bonus." He tapped on one of the stones in the wall and it creaked open. The cubby was filled with vials, jars and various small velvet bags. He grabbed a jar filled with what looked like tiny blue bath beads and shook them where the floor met the walls.

"Each bead is absorbent enough to swallow a moat."

"I might have to hit her up for some of those. It would be an awesome addition to my kill bag." Small powerful magic was ideal when killing demons on-the-go.

Giovani smiled and squeezed her shoulder. This was a sign of affection reserved for men, which made her love him more. He truly respected her, and more importantly, he was one of the few people living that she desired approval from.

"You're practical, like your mother," Giovani said. "So few demons have common sense these days." He returned to the hidden chamber, put the empty jar away, then picked up two vials. One was a murky green and the other was the color of scorched earth. "The fun part was gathering their essences without being detected."

Scarlett raised her eyebrow. That sounded gross.

"Kings get bored too, and no, it's not something nasty like that. Kali enjoys her CSI work on the Earthly Realm. You'd be amazed what she can concoct from a few cells. All she needs is a smidge of DNA to create summoning potions."

Scarlett chose the murky green vial, which held Silvia's essence. Aracana's reptilian lover was a pleasure to look at, when out of biting reach. "Most men of your generation resist technology, and here you are, using human science for witchcraft. Total genius."

He smiled, soaking in the compliment. "On second thought, I think we should call my sister first. It will piss her off to watch her beloved be summoned by her own niece." Giovani spilled the matte black powder in the center of the room, away from wood and other pliable natural objects. His sister could animate just about anything, all she needed to do was touch it. Thankfully, the stones the tower was built with could only be activated by Giovani. He had studied stone masonry during one of his teenage rebellions, before he became king.

The powder hardened into a spike that grew tall enough to touch the ceiling. Black smoke swirled around the deadly wooden spire. The room grew parched like a dry riverbed in the desert. Arcana didn't have fire magic, but she was a master of earthly things: living, dead, and undead. The smoke was dense and morphed into the body of a woman. Arcana's skirt reminded Scarlett of dense spider webs. Her aunt wore a corset made from the skin of an American beech tree. The stiff silvery bark was so confining that Scarlett felt sympathetic shortness of breath.

Arcana was beautifully terrifying, like the free fall before crashing onto rocks frothy with ocean waves. She could make death exquisite, an art form Scarlett could appreciate. Many of Cane's lovers had perished this way.

But Auntie Cane wasn't all sugar and dreamy poison. She liked to watch her enemies suffer. She'd kill them only to bring them back again for a fresh wave of torture. Some deaths lasted centuries, until she lost her patience. Which was right about the time electricity was discovered. She resented the end of pitch-black night.

The tattoo on her forehead kept changing shape, each design more haunting than the last. Mesmerism was one of her strong suits.

"Auntie Cane, what a pleasure to see you again."

"You always told pretty lies."

Scarlett pushed back the feeling of spikes entering

her skull. To say Cane's mind riding was invasive was like saying a volcano was a tad hot.

"I'm glad Belladonna tricked you with hers. It was a pleasure to watch you twist in the wind. All those tears…" Cane licked her lips as if Scarlett's despair was a delicacy.

Giovani was not amused. He surrounded his sister with flames. The heat melted Cane's mascara, which left veins of black dripping down her cheeks. The fire dissipated with a thunderclap. Scarlett was gratified when her aunt jumped, singeing her dark red hair.

"Milkman, iz not rainin'. Whyz there thunder?"

Cane's eyes were drawn to the sound of Magnolia's voice. The greed and avarice was unmistakable; she was a part of this. Be that as it may, Giovani did not imprison people for their thoughts, only their deeds. The dungeons would never be able to accommodate all the demons with impure thoughts. Moreover, he required evidence of wrongdoing before he meted out punishment. "Have you been making friends, sister?"

Cane's voice was captivating, and no matter what she said, it felt beautiful. Scarlett was fascinated by its darkness. Even murder sounded like honey from her lips. "I don't make friends." There was a dark shimmer in her black eyes.

For dramatic effect, Scarlett dropped her vial. The air above the solution transformed into a column of water. The water shimmered with living things, snakes and eels. The aquatic cocktail morphed into a Siren, a mermaid with no tail. Her feet were bare and blended in with the stone floor, like a chameleon.

Scarlett could feel her aunt's anger. It was potent and dark, impossible to ignore.

Giovani paid no attention to the newest guest and returned to Cane's claim of being friendless. "Of course not. You have always been a *sour* sister."

Silvia hissed. She made fury sexy. Her lips glistened pink like conch shells, and her skin had the hue of scales without the deformity. Her wicked green eyes were true reptilian, with dark slashes down the center like a dragon. "Why have you summoned us? Has your toy gone away to play suck face with other men? Succubae are incapable of fidelity."

Her father didn't rise to the bait. Giovani was fascinated by the lovers like a guest in a lethal aquarium. He had gotten all he needed from this meeting when Cane displayed her tell. Scarlett was disappointed that her aunt had made her power lust so obvious. She had been hoping for a game of cat and mouse, or in this case shark and minnow.

"It's been a pleasure. You can go now." Giovani dismissed his sister.

"Family reunion over so soon? I'm crushed." Cane looked like she'd love to crush every bone in Giovani's body.

"Crushed you say?" With a wave of his hand, he threw the two women together with such velocity that bones did break and shatter.

Silvia's rage released a fountain of water that gushed outward and soaked the walls. Scarlett giggled when the wee blue spheres rose to absorb the water, like a fish being fed in a tank. "That is *so* cool!"

Cane's wrists expelled thorny vines that swirled around Scarlett's body. Which was also way cool. They burst into flames when they came in contact with her protective shields. She hadn't been attacked this way in years. Scarlett sent a wave of fire to surround the women. Silvia's skin was sizzling and Cane's skirt began to smolder. As much as she was enjoying this little spat, time was short. She cast a banishing spell. There was a pile of gross left behind. "Look, a bouquet of roses for Kali. She'll be so pleased."

"Like I said, kiddo, I love your sense of humor."

Chapter Thirty-two

"I have had e-fucking-nough of your self-absorbed bullshit." Lilith had cornered Tia in the kitchen. Each doorway out was electrified. No one was going to interrupt this third come-to-Jesus meeting. Lilith wanted to rip Tia's heart out because that's exactly what Tia had done to her. Her first meaningful kiss, the first person to ever love her back, was interrupted by Tia's drama. On top of losing her shit and smacking Sinister Scarlett, Tia had broken the rules along with the mirror into Magnolia's nursery.

Now that Kayla was gone with her shadow Pandora, Lilith had reached the very end of her rope. "You're supposed to be a picture-perfect mom, which was annoying at times, but it was something everyone could count on. What the fuck with your temper tantrums?" When Tia looked like she would mouth off, Lilith stopped her. "Explain yourself and how you plan to fix this."

Tia smoldered for a few moments. Lilith tapped her electric blue stiletto nails on the table, creating tiny sparks. She wanted to gouge the wooden surface, but refrained. She wouldn't waste her claws on a table when what she really wanted was her pound of flesh.

Tia's silence was pissing her off. The others in the house tried to break through the barriers, but they sizzled like bugs in a zapper. Luke and Beau were raising quite the ruckus at the base of the stairs, but she didn't give a fuck. Winter the Uptight was stupidly testing the doorway to the hallway, and Sophia was pressing her luck at the back door. They would all fail. Lilith didn't have a bad attitude, she was the real thing, crackling with lightning and poised to strike. "Now Tia, man up!" She slapped the table.

Tia seemed to measure her words. "At first I thought it had to do with Magnolia and fear of what my father would do to her." She fussed with her red curls. Lilith was going to scalp the bitch if she didn't get to the good part soon. "Then I realized it was *The Darkness*."

"You set us up!" Lilith stood, her hands filled with balls of lightning. "You tried to kill Kayla and Luke. What the fuck?" Living here was now like a funhouse, disturbing and surreal.

"Please sit down. You asked me to explain, now you need to listen to what I have to say. If you still want to waste me when I finish, be my guest. I have nothing left to lose."

"But Magnolia does." Lilith extinguished the blue fire that licked at her fingertips. "I didn't figure you for a coward. Talk. Cut the touchy-feely crap. I'm so not in the mood."

"Fair enough." Tia tamed her hair into a bun. She looked around the room as if she didn't want her family to witness what she was about to say. "Mama, Luke, Beau, Winter. I need you to leave us alone." There was a chorus of protests, but they obeyed her command, for now. Tia gripped her green tea mug. The liquid had to be bitter and stone cold, which Lilith found fitting.

Tia hissed out a breath, then started her dark tale with a dead voice. "I had nothing to do with *The Darkness* that stalked you kids."

Lilith resented the characterization, but kept her silence out of curiosity.

"I have a feeling that *The Darkness* came from my family, though I don't know who specifically other than my half-brother Rayne. He's dead and was far from leader material. Someone put him up to what happened. Kayla and Luke's attempted murder, and Angel's death." Tears slipped from her eyes, but she didn't bother to wipe them away. "*The Darkness* that has now surfaced came from my blood. I'm half demon."

"Whoa." Tia just got more interesting. Lilith didn't know why she hadn't made the connection earlier—of course she was half demon.

"I have worked my entire life to stay in the light and share it with others. In my arrogance, I thought I had overcome my blood. That Father had no power over me. No meaningful connection to my life." The chair scraped as Tia stood up. She emptied her cup of tea and poured a fresh one. Tia drank enough to wet her lips then rested the mug on the island—the exact place where Tia ejected Kayla from Lilith's life. They may not have been girlfriends the way Lilith had hoped, but at least she could be close, and love her from a distance. Bitterness burned into fury within her soul. She stood to avoid setting the chair on fire.

Tia flinched, but made no move to protect herself. "Magnolia's capture ignited my rage. It was a modest fire with potential for more." Her hands had been loose at her sides when she started her story, now her fingertips were going white from her grip on the counter. "I tried to shove it down and swallow my pride when Scarlett showed up."

"That pasty bitch oozes darkness."

The scent of lilacs filled the room. Lilith couldn't understand why the floral fragrance was putting Tia on edge. "Step away from the island before you rip the counter off," Lilith ordered.

Tia obeyed. "Mama wore lilac perfume when we lived in Giovani's castle. She emptied the perfume bottles and left behind the candles. She hates lilacs now. They remind her of Father."

"Did he hurt her?" Lilith couldn't stand the thought of Sophia being beaten or harmed.

Tia shook her head. "Giovani loved her, but Sophia hated the darkness in him and the violence it brought into their lives. He didn't try to stop her when she left, he understood." The tea had cooled enough for Tia to knock it back in one shot. "Rage filled me when Scarlett rode Magnolia's memories. She's my baby, I deserved to—"

"Cut the entitlement crap, you slapped her hard enough to leave a handprint. It would have bruised if she hadn't healed herself." Self-healing was rad, and if she hadn't been so pissed at Scarlett for dragging drama to their doorstep, they would have been friends. Scarlett knew things Lilith actually wanted to learn. Spy and assassin, two jobs Lilith would relish. She never fit in with the sugary sweet goodness in this damn house, except with Angel. That was another loss she wanted to avenge. The foot soldiers were dead, but the mastermind was still up for grabs.

"The rage and anger was like poison. I don't know how to temper it and function the way Scarlett and Giovani do." Tia grimaced at that confession. "I don't know how to be bad and honorable at the same time. All I have now is rage."

The air in the room was stifling. The herbs and

plants grew at an unnatural pace, and they sucked in oxygen rather than creating it. Lilith could feel the benign plants go toxic. "Dial it down a notch before you create a dark jungle."

Tia took deep calming breaths. Demi, Sophia's girlfriend, had taught them how to meditate and center themselves. "I wish Demi was here. I can't seem to take the edge off, even when I try."

"Enough of the *Namaste* shit. We need to put your dark energy to work."

"I will kill myself before I go evil." Tia's green eyes glowed like creepy lanterns. The housemother was sure getting more fascinating by the moment.

"Who said anything about evil?" Lilith crafted a boomerang from blue flame then tossed it. The object broke into a million tiny sparks when she caught it on the rebound. "You need to purge the anger from your system. Doing magic always takes the edge off mine. Wield it against those who deserve their fate. We need to go after them." Lilith murmured a few words and the blue zappers extinguished, allowing the family access to the kitchen.

"Amen to that. I'm done with waiting on Scarlett," Tia said.

"You hated being on the other end of the rules. It's easier to make them than follow them."

"Guilty as charged. Why don't we formulate a plan together?"

Sophia breezed in and kissed Tia on the top of her head. "There's my girl."

"'Bout time." Beau expressed his approval and followed it up with a hug. "I can scry for the girls, but I want to hold off on Magnolia. We need to beat this as a team then bring our little girl home."

"Somehow I think Magnolia will do her fair share of vanquishing," Lilith said with pride.

Tia tensed, but she seemed to accept this change. Regardless of Magnolia's size, her little girl wasn't a little girl anymore. "I don't like it, but I know you're right."

Lilith couldn't wait to see what that little badass could do. She wished she had been around to watch Magnolia blast a hole through her uncle's chest instead of settling for Beau's PG description. The young avenger got her own slice of justice on Angel's behalf. They were a few bodies short of total revenge. Lilith would enjoy watching the demons get bagged and tagged. *Let the bodies hit the floor.*

Chapter Thirty-three

Of course Maxim, a man of luxe drama, had to have a home with footpath-only access. The climb up the cliff was harrowing for anyone not petite and under five feet tall. Yet, she managed.

"Peas let me down, I can walk," Magnolia needled for the third time in the past five minutes.

"Sweetie, I know you can walk and run really fast, but this is a dangerous path, and I want to be sure you are safe."

"Why I not safe with No-no?"

Scarlett was huffing a bit. She may be in shape, but Magnolia wasn't exactly willing cargo. She regretted her desire for a challenge; this wasn't what she had in mind. "Jonah has been dishonest with us and we don't know who he's been working for. It has to be someone in the castle." She didn't dumb down her answer. Magnolia may use baby talk, but she was *way* older than Scarlett soul-wise. "We need to pick up Kayla and Pandora."

"Oh, I loves Kaywa. And you know Dora the Explorer too!" Unfortunately, Magnolia clapped her hands with delight. Carrying her was like wrestling with an eel.

"Pandora is a real girl, she's the latest foster. She's been having a rough go of it. Your mother's been a bit batty and scared Pandora." Scarlett didn't want to share the whole scoop, but Pandora and Kayla were bound to fill her in.

"Oh no! I makes happy. I makes Kaywa and Pandora happy. When can I makes Mama happy again?"

Magnolia's red hair was fluffy like cotton candy. Scarlett had to resist the desire to spit out the locks that tickled her lips. "That may take time, but we'll have a sleepover at my house. Did I mention I know how to make chocolate chip cookies?"

Scarlett was intensely relieved to see the cave entrance. Excited Magnolia was literally getting too hot to handle.

"No-no told you my favorite! Hurray!" The child was a living exclamation point.

"Hold still a moment, Magnolia. There are lots of tricks on the way to Maxim's home. So no running ahead. The tricks and traps keep the bad people out, but could hurt you accidentally."

Magnolia sucked in her lower lip as she considered this bit of information. "I trust you Vanilla Sissy."

Scarlett snickered. She'd take that over Milkman any day. Scarlett was sorry to leave her father and cousins behind. They were in extraordinary danger, much worse than the usual court intrigue. Flushing out the traitor was normally Scarlett's job, but protecting Magnolia trumped all other responsibilities. She was actually glad when Father suggested she take Magnolia out of the castle. One, it meant that she didn't need to snatch her, and two, she didn't want her father to think she didn't trust him to keep Magnolia safe.

"Magnolia, let me check your sneaker laces. I want to make sure they are nice and tight." She rested Magnolia on a ledge and checked to be sure that her sneakers were secure. It had taken a good fifteen minutes to talk Magnolia out of the tutu and crown she wanted to wear on this trip. She tucked Magnolia's shirt into her pants, and made sure the belt would hold them up. The toddler had been so good that Scarlett rewarded her with a little toss in the air, which of course gave her niece the giggles.

"Again, again!"

Scarlett inhaled sharply. She regretted the impetuous move. "Once we're safe, I promise I will toss you again."

Magnolia wasn't pleased, but to Scarlett's relief she didn't make a fuss.

Scarlett kissed her on her cute freckled nose. "Ready for Maxim's kooky cave?"

"Oh I can't wait to see my Kaywa. Let's go, slowpoke."

Their journey was filled with hair-raising switchbacks between narrow pathways. It had never bothered Scarlett before. She usually enjoyed the challenge. Getting Magnolia to keep her promise of taking it slow was terrifying at moments. Her bestie loved to change the safe path, especially if he felt his lair had been accessed by undesirables. She didn't know why he bothered, as unwelcome guests always perished. Scarlett was pretty sure Maxim liked his guests dazed and confused upon arrival.

Magnolia had reached the end of her patience when their goal was in sight. Maxim opened the massive oak door, for what he had intended to be a grand welcome, but the squirt barreled past him and jumped into Kayla's arms.

"Don't cry Kaywa, everything will be okay." The little girl put her pudgy hands on Kayla's cheeks and gave her a big smacking kiss on the lips. "I makes you happy. Scarlett pomised we could make chocolate chip cookies at her house."

"She did, did she?" Kayla looked over Magnolia's head at Scarlett. She seemed wary, but not completely pissed off. Scarlett was pretty sure the healthy bubbly toddler jabbering in her arms was the reason why.

"Oh yes, I loves No-no, and Jet has no colors, just like Scarlett. I told him Jet was a silly name so I call him Milkman instead."

No way, Maxim mouthed.

Scarlett's smile was wicked. "There is enough photographic evidence to bribe or shame him for centuries. Maxim, he let her color him with markers and even convinced him to sit down for a tea party."

"Milkman was in charge of the milk," Magnolia said with zest.

Vivian emerged from the shadows, her amusement was a bit vampire creepy, but Scarlett didn't mind. She figured her mother had been bored senseless for years. These weeks had been unpredictable and dangerous, a flavor of fun they both savored. "Darling, come inside and eat something. Maxim has been cooking for hours," Vivian said.

"No, he just waved his arms," Pandora protested. Her sourpuss showed she was less than impressed with this turn of events. Magnolia had stolen Kayla's undivided attention. If Scarlett was a better person, she would have empathized with the tween, but seeing Pandora turn green was too much fun to soften.

"Vivian, I hope he prepared your favorite meal."

Her mother mimed using a toothpick. "Delivered on arrival."

"Excellent, let's eat. I've earned an entire chocolate cake for surviving your maze with this impatient firestarter spurring me on." The adrenaline high from their escape and arrival was ebbing. She needed fuel. Scarlett ate so much her belly paunched. "Look Maxim, I made a food baby!"

Magnolia looked alarmed and pushed her plate away. "I don't wanna make babies."

That gave Scarlett and Kayla the giggles. "Not a for-real baby, just a little tummy," Scarlett managed between gasps of laughter.

Magnolia plumped out her lower lip. She didn't like being laughed at.

"No pouting honey, we're laughing because you made us happy." Scarlett reveled in the lighthearted moment.

"See Kaywa, I told you I makes you happy. You too, Pan-dora. Here, have a cookie," Magnolia said as she passed the sweet treat to Pandora, which earned her a reluctant smile.

A shadow crossed Kayla's face, as if a cloud of sadness blocked her joy. Scarlett wondered what she was thinking about, but wouldn't ask. She was about to tease a smile out of Kayla when Magnolia made her laugh again.

Sometimes happy memories can make you sad, Maxim spoke into her mind. *Kayla's whole again. You did a good thing bringing Magnolia here.*

"Daughter, thank you for livening things up," Vivian said as she rose from the table. "I'm off to do my good deed."

Maxim smirked. "Is that what they are calling it these days?"

To Scarlett's great surprise, Vivian blushed. Maybe there was still hope for her parents. It would never be a deep love like Giovani felt for Sophia, but it would be an honest one.

Scarlett embraced her mother and walked her out. She handed Vivian the bag of gold coins Giovani gave her earlier. "Don't spend it all in one place." She kissed her mother on both cheeks and hugged her goodbye.

"Don't be silly, I will spend it in many places. Rodeo Drive is calling my name."

"Make those saleswomen work for it."

"I'll give 'em hell and they will love every minute of it." Vivian sashayed down the first of many trails. The world was her runway.

Chapter Thirty-four

"What the hell happened?" Lilith demanded. Beau was able to call back Kayla and Pandora's escape, the human DVR that he was, but when it came to the part where they got company, the image blurred. She could see Pandora's shock and Kayla's dismay at the new arrival. The person or being was obscured by smoke. She couldn't tell if it was male or female, skinny or fat...nothing. "I'm not seeing what I'm seeing."

Beau replied with a cheeky, "That's completely up to you. Though it's pretty badass to conjure up the dead."

"I had no idea she had progressed that far," Tia added in wonder as the ghostly apparitions grew in number. Their menacing shapes were clear and the ghosts appeared to be looking to Pandora for guidance.

"Don't see as how you could have managed that, with your head so far up your ass," Lilith said with a growl. Her homicidal desires had muted but still lingered. She wouldn't relish harming Tia, but she wasn't going to pull any punches either.

Sophia was as captivated as the others in the room, but her full-on grandma mode remained intact. She rested her hand on Lilith's shoulder and spoke softly, "Language Lilith, and I don't mean your curses. Words are powerful things and you are hurting my daughter." Sophia gazed at Tia as she continued. "We need to be kind to each other and work as a team. That can't happen if you are constantly verbally slashing at each other." Sophia's green eyes were soft and nonjudgmental. "We are all hurting, let's be sure we focus our displeasure on the enemy. Tearing each other down will only make their job easier."

Lilith rocked her tongue ring from side to side within her closed mouth. She knew Sophia was right. She wasn't going to apologize, but would keep what Sophia said in mind.

Lilith's thoughts were suspended as she saw the huge net snare Kayla and Pandora. Her horror turned to rage as the two were bound. The silky slither of the blindfolds pushed her over the edge. "I'm going to kill that bitch."

"What if it's a boy?" Beau asked.

Beau was trying to lighten the mood, but that was so not happening. "Then I'll make him my bitch."

It must have been stress because Lilith's comment gave the siblings the giggles. Tia was more the punch drunk of the two. Lilith was not amused, and she was tempted to dig her sharp nails into their soft vulnerable throats. "Can you follow where they were taken?"

Beau strained, beads of sweat dripped down his face. Tia took her brother's hand and lent him her support along with a healing boost; Tia could amplify the powers of those around her. The effort didn't do any good since the pathway was as blacked out as the kidnapper.

Lilith wanted to throw or shred something. Flesh or wood, both would do the trick. "What about Magnolia?"

The mirror rippled and revealed Magnolia in the tower nursery, the place they had taken her after Rayne-the-fuckup's attack. Lilith narrowed her eyes when she saw Magnolia's pale-skinned playmate. "What is it with you guys and your freaky white friends?"

Tia's anger made her aura pulse. She was not pleased. "Scarlett left my daughter in the care of a fucking executioner! Since when are warlords babysitter material?"

"I'm going to punt that bitch where it hurts," Lilith threatened. The rage grew inside her. She knew the cocky colorless killer couldn't be trusted.

Beau got the giggles again, but Lilith had no idea what had him laughing. She could barely see through the red haze of her anger. When Winter and Sophia started laughing, she dialed it down a notch.

"You have no colors, I gives you colors," Magnolia offered. *"Jet is a mean name. I call you Milkman because you look like skim milk."* The toddler picked up a box of markers. *"I can give you colors."*

The young man looked pained and amused at the same time.

"Oh my God!" Beau was beside himself. "She's not only got him playing tea party, she gave him a tutu to wear as a crown."

Lilith chuckled as the muscle bound idiot was bossed around by a child barely three feet tall. "Magnolia is a badass. Wasting Rayne was rad, but bossing around the White Chocolate Prince...totally priceless."

The tension in Tia's shoulders eased, but it was clear she was not happy. Her dismay seemed to quickly shift to anger when Scarlett entered the nursery. This time, the magical blur tool blackened out the trio.

Seconds later, Magnolia and Scarlett were gone and Jet was trying to wash off his "colors."

"What's the deal with the magical Photoshop?" Lilith suspected that the blur that captured Kayla and Pandora was related to Scarlett. "Beau, any chance you picked up where they went off to?"

Beau shook his head. "Some demons can cover their tracks. If Scarlett didn't want to us to see where they were going, it's a done deal."

Luke, who had been quiet from the moment he entered the kitchen, piped up. "Just because it looks bad, doesn't mean it is bad."

"Since when are you an expert on anything?" Lilith snapped.

Beau waved his hand over the shimmering surface, returning it to ordinary water in a black bowl. Apparently the show was over. "We need to listen to each other, Lilith. Even if you don't agree, you have to hear him out. Luke's a person with feelings, just like anyone else in this house."

Lilith clenched her jaw then clacked the metal ball at the end of her tongue ring against her front teeth. If she wasn't going to cut Tia some slack, she certainly wasn't going to listen to Moody Model Boy, but Lilith would let them think she was listening.

Luke leaned against the fridge so he could see everyone in the room. "The blur may be as frustrating as not knowing, but have you considered the reason behind the mystery?" No one offered answers. "What if she is blocking the bad guys and not us?"

Beau took up for Luke. "Exactly. What if the blurs are people making sure Kayla, Pandora, and Magnolia are safe? You can't selectively block with a cloaking spell that strong."

"Beau, I know you like Scarlett, but I think your affection is blinding you to an undeniable truth." Tia's outrage was a living thing. Lilith could almost taste her anger. She liked this version of Tia much better than her Mary Poppins act. "Scarlett had my baby, took her out of the castle, but did not bring her home."

Beau didn't know what to say to that.

Luke wasn't having it. "Scarlett didn't have to heal me or help me unblock my powers, and she didn't have to include me to make the potion to break the aging curse." Luke's calm surprised Lilith. He was usually a brat when things didn't go his way, which was pretty much all of the time. "Scarlett had nothing to gain from those things. If Giovani, with all his powers couldn't secure her safety, how they hell could we?"

"Enough," Tia said. "Don't you dare tell me that I can't protect my baby." She squared her shoulders and glared at Beau and Luke. "Even if Scarlett had my kid's best interests at heart, she has no right to make unilateral decisions."

Lilith tilted her head. "Give it to me straight. Are you pissed because you think she's doing wrong by Magnolia, or is this just another symptom of your resentment that an eighteen-year-old is calling the shots?" That one was a direct hit. Lilith had sunk her battleship.

"It's not like that. I don't trust her." Tia was adamant, but Lilith knew it was bullshit, which actually worked in her favor. She wanted to take that pasty bitch down and make her suffer for all the hurt she brought into Lilith's life.

Lilith decided to push her agenda. "Blind faith has gotten us nowhere. Beau and Luke, you can sit back and wait for the assassin to phone home. I'm done waiting. Tia, you ready to get your baby back?"

"Yes." It was only one word, but it was spoken with feeling.

Lilith knew the softies in the room weren't on board, which was for the best. Tia was more likely to let her dark side come out and play without witnesses. "If you aren't with us, fine. Just stay the fuck out of our way."

Chapter Thirty-five

"If you knew how to do this, why on earth did you let Scarlett call the shots?" Lilith was still not tracking.

"Dark magic. I have steered clear of it all my life." Tia hopped a bit to readjust her heavy backpack. They were standing in the last place Kayla and Pandora had been spotted.

Lilith was a bit annoyed with Tia, but happier that she had chosen action over feeling sorry for herself. "Common sense, Tia. By avoiding this part of yourself, you have made yourself vulnerable." Lilith used a blue fireball to light their way. It was kind of bizarre that the kidnapper took the packs and sleeping bag when snatching them up. "You were always harping on us about not keeping things bottled up and how to find balance. What gives?"

Tia was blunt. "Arrogance, hubris."

Lilith raised a sculpted blue eyebrow, knowing that Tia was holding back.

Tia shrugged. "And yes, a lack of common sense."

Lilith snorted. Tia's honesty was a refreshing change. "Do you sense anything?"

Tia ran her hand over the place where the girls had been sleeping and did the same for the area blurred in the vision. She bit the corner of her lip. "Something is familiar. Do you smell perfume?"

Lilith offered her wrist. "Is it me?"

"Not quite, but close." Tia walked the crime scene, this time comically sniffing everything. Her nose nearly touched the cement walkway and the steel beams holding up the bridge, as she tried to place the fragrance.

A spike rose up from the embankment. Tia was too busy playing bloodhound to sense the danger. "Tia, I think we're about to have company." Lilith made sure her knives were in easy reach and braced herself. The dark smoke circling the spike was freaky. "Tia!" Lilith's shout made a sharp report, not unlike a gunshot. She finally got Tia's attention.

Tia dropped her pack and rushed to Lilith's side. The bottom of the dark cloud shifted into a nest of black cobwebs as the length of the spike swirled into the form of a woman. The woman appeared with a black cowl obscuring her face, and when she tipped her head back the cowl drifted to her shoulders. She looked eerily like a taller, more imposing version of Tia: long red hair, sharp emerald eyes, and a tribal tattoo on her forehead. The black tattoo shifted into different haunting shapes, each new configuration more ominous than the last. Whoever this bitch was, her makeup was on point from her smoky coal-lined eyes to her blood-red lipstick.

"Arcana," Tia mumbled. The name itself made Tia's energy cave inward.

Great, I guess I am in charge of not getting us killed. Lilith was up for a rumble. Blue sparks radiated from her long, sharp nails as her eyes swirled an electric blue.

Arcana repressed a smile. "Irony my dear, will it ever leave me be? I loathe electricity and yet here I am, staring at the living embodiment of that wretched invention, polluting night with her blue sparks."

Another woman slithered into view. She had the body of a belly dancer. Her full hips were covered by green scales that wafted outward like a gypsy skirt—that is, if gypsies wore live garments. Her feet were bare and blended into the color of the earth beneath her. The woman's stomach was faintly rounded and accented by a belly ring. Scales covered her breasts, and curiously, the color of the scales continued from the tops of her breasts to the skin of her face, but instead of scales, her skin was smooth. "You bitches know how to dress."

"Lilith!" Tia was clearly shocked by her comment.

"You tell me language and I will rip out your tongue," Lilith warned. She was done with Tia's Pollyanna bullshit.

"My dear niece, it seems that your taste in companions has improved," Arcana complimented. "Her magic is unfortunate, but her fashion sense is delicious." She directed her next comment at Lilith. "Maybe we can go shopping once this dreary business is taken care of."

Lilith grinned. She needed more evil in her life, and she suspected Fish Girl and Spider Spooky were her kind of crazy. "Tia, is every killer a member of your family?"

Tia was still stuck on stupid, so Lilith decided to take control of the situation. "I'm Lilith, and apparently you are Arcana, and the aquatic bint is…?"

Mermaid-meets-python laughed and apprised Lilith's outfit from head to toe. "I'm Silvia."

Silvia's voice gave Lilith a delicious shiver. There was no doubt about it, these evil beings were "family" of the lesbian variety. She liked them even more. "Don't tell me, let me guess, you are here to help?"

"Tia darling, did she rip your tongue out so quickly that I missed it? If so, brava." Arcana clapped. "Otherwise, pipe up."

That snapped Tia out of her shocked silence. "Aunt, Silvia, I have no idea what to say or who to trust for that matter. Did you snatch up the girls? Are we next?"

Silvia's laugh was pleasant, like water in babbling brook. "No we didn't snatch Firefly and I-see-dead-people. I saw their snares, but not their captor."

Maybe Luke was right and the blur was meant to block all eyes, since these two ladies didn't bat for the light team. She couldn't deny their chemistry. Tia may be freaking out, but Lilith was happy with this turn of events. They were obviously after the same quarry and Tia's ability to work dark magic was spotty at best. "Why do you care?"

Arcana answered. "Giovani has overstepped his bounds. He snatched up my grand-niece to get at her powers and has been summoning us for sport." Dark anger smoldered in her eyes and the air smelled like a torched forest. "He hasn't eaten her soul or consumed her powers, *yet*. But I think Rayne-the-fuckup has forced his hand. Magnolia is being kept in a tower."

Lilith lost a little faith in the duo who were one step behind. "They're not in the tower anymore."

"That's what dear Scarlett wants us to believe."

This was a definite possibility. Misdirection was a common tactical strategy.

"Even if you're right, there's no breaking into that tower and you know it." Tia's rage was disturbing the air around her. Dead leaves, trash, and dirt-encrusted pebbles trembled and scratched the cement at her feet.

"If he's desperate, we need get her now."

Arcana smiled with perfect white teeth. The incisors looked sharp, and Lilith wondered if she had dental work to make her appear like a vampire. Many of her Goth friends had done so. Though considering who she was dealing with, piercing skin and drinking blood probably wasn't a lifestyle choice. "We have a way into the tower, a traitor has access. Once we get the girl, we will deal with Giovani for good."

"You're going to murder your brother?" Tia's voice went up at the end.

Silvia hissed. "Tia, cut the crap. Especially since you long to do the deed yourself."

Tia's eyes gleamed like green lanterns. The truth was there. Lilith was actually proud of Tia. She was all for killing the fucker who set this entire mess in motion. If the asshole hadn't nabbed Magnolia, Kayla wouldn't be lost. She'd be at home and they would be together. "If you know how to get Magnolia, why do you need us? What's in it for you?"

Arcana flashed her a smile, her sharp teeth were definitely the real McCoy. "I need your help to kill Giovani. Magnolia's red fire mixed with your blue can scorch a hole through my brother's stronghold. Together you can end him."

Silvia's reptilian eyes were disturbing and really cool. The dark slash down the middle was so metal. Lilith was digging it and her. Arcana seemed catch that thought and surprised Lilith with a knowing grin. *Willing to share, interesting.* Lilith's decision was made. "I'm ready for a snatch and torch, but what about Kayla and Pandora?"

"Magnolia will light the way," Arcana promised.

Chapter Thirty-six

Scarlett's heart rate kicked up a notch. There was a mixture of power in the air, a twisted tornado of dark and light magic. She knew deep in her heart that her sister had made a decision, one as potentially lethal as Tia's desire to give up her life. The scent of scorched earth and the reek of rancid fish confirmed her suspicions.

Magnolia slid from Kayla's arms onto the floor, her small body pulsing with white magic. The light was nearly blinding. When she spoke, there was not one ounce of baby talk in her tone, which made it all the more terrifying and heartbreaking. Her old soul was in complete control now. "Mother and Lilith, they are in danger. Cane and Silvia have injected poison into their hearts. They are casting their lot with the true *Darkness*."

Having her fears confirmed made Scarlett nauseous. "Tia doesn't know how to control *The Darkness* and Lilith is being seduced by the opportunity to let her rage come out to play. *The Darkness*, it was Cane and Silvia all along." Scarlett couldn't believe she'd missed it. Yes, the sound of Magnolia's voice had revealed Cane's desire for Magnolia's power, but that was only a fraction of the bigger picture. "She's going to turn them evil and tear Father's heart out in the process. Oh my God, and Sophia's too. How could I have been so blind?"

Magnolia drew some of the light back into herself. Scarlett was waiting for her to change form, but her body kept its true age. "They never intended to kill me, I was the distraction. I was the bait to bring Mother here, and Lilith as well."

The heat in the room was intense enough to melt the candles on the table, but it wasn't Scarlett or Magnolia's doing. Kayla's eyes were filled with swirling angry flames. There was no iris or pupil, only fire. "I will kill them before they get the chance. No one is taking Lilith from me."

Magnolia's voice was deeper and deadly serious. "They can't have my mother either."

"Finally," Maxim praised. "Finally you've gotten your shit together."

Scarlett glared at her friend. "You knew this was going to happen and you didn't bother to tell me?"

Maxim rolled his eyes. "Seriously, dial down the crazy. No, I did not know this was going to happen. Why on earth would I want all your fierce estrogen in my home? That goes for all of you, not just Scarlett." He looked truly offended. "I prefer my catfights and blood drama on *The Real Housewives*. I hate having guests in my home. I'm a fucking hermit for Christ's sake. The quicker you get this shit handled, the better. I've seen more of you in the last few weeks than I have in the past three years."

Scarlett ruffled his hair because she really wanted to and it would piss him off. His reaction was as expected. She reached into her back pocket and pulled out her smartphone. She scrolled through her call log and hit redial. "Mother, I hope you haven't gone far."

The sound of honking horns and girly chatter meant that her mother was already shopping. "Darling dear, no grass grows under my feet. Speaking of feet, I just bought the most darling pair of high heels. The stems look strong enough to pierce through flesh and bone." Scarlett chuckled at how Mother was always considering how an accessory could be weaponized. Bless her heart.

"Cane and Silvia have sunk their teeth into Tia and Lilith."

Kayla growled. Fire licked at her fingertips. Scarlett waved her hand and quashed the flames. No need to set Maxim's lair on fire.

The playfulness in her mother's banter shifted to cold calculation. "I may need help if I am to murder them both, but it's a challenge I've longed to take on."

Scarlett smiled. She really loved her mother. "I need you to track and keep an eye on them. Murder Cane and Silvia if you must, but no harm can come to my sister or Lilith."

Kayla was close to blowing her top, and that wasn't an option. "Kayla, chill. Vivian will track them while we formulate a plan. You'll be able to get your human-torch on later."

Kayla lunged in Scarlett's direction, but Magnolia stopped her cold. "Kayla, she is not your enemy. Let her do her job." Kayla hung back, but she wasn't happy.

"Text me if you need backup," Scarlett offered, but her mother had already hung up. Vivian never wasted time on pleasantries and Scarlett appreciated that. Each moment Tia and Lilith were with the Twisted Trysters they were turning darker. Soon evil would cease to feel foreign. They had to get to Tia and Lilith before it was too late.

"Maxim, keep an eye on the women. I want to avoid telling Father for as long as possible. The traitors in the castle can't know that their plans have been exposed. It might force their hand. Father may think he's invulnerable, but anything that lives can be murdered."

Chapter Thirty-seven

Liquid silver the size of a pea appeared and grew larger. Scarlett automatically pushed Magnolia behind her. "Kayla, be ready with some fire power. Creating a portal in Maxim's home is either a suicide mission or the caster is extremely powerful."

When the guests materialized, Magnolia walked through Scarlett's legs and barreled into Beau. "Silly boy you must be vewy powerful to come here. Scarlett says so."

It lifted Scarlett's heart to hear the childlike language from her lips. It seems Magnolia's old soul only took over when necessary.

Beau lifted the delighted cherub. The family resemblance was obvious from their fiery red hair to their emerald green eyes. "Little munchkin, I have missed you like crazy."

Magnolia clapped her hands and squealed. "Are you here to play hide and seek?"

Scarlett pursed her lips then smirked. Their mission sort of qualified. "Yeah, Carrot Top, you ready to find my sissy and Lilith fair?"

Luke made his presence known through a bout of hysterical laughter. "I. Can't. Even," he exclaimed.

Scarlett was baffled. "What are you laughing at?"

"Sissy and Lilith Fair." Luke gasped. "I don't know why, but that just cracked me up. Leave me alone, it's been a long day."

"Everybody has laughin' here and happy." Magnolia was so cute Scarlett wanted to squish her. Baby talk was much more welcome than that of the fearsome warrior.

Maxim tapped his foot, but didn't look sincerely pissed. "Beau, you sexy beast. How on earth did you manage to break into my lair?"

Beau showed the small puncture wound on his fingertip. "Blood magic, of course. Besides, little miss thing was a blast of white light. We couldn't have missed her if we tried."

"Fuck." Scarlett was not thrilled. She texted her mother and was pleased that the motley crew was too far from Maxim's to see that particular light show. "Mother's tracking them and Cane's way too cocky to spot her tail."

Beau chortled. "Slithering Silvia's tail is the only one she pays attention to. As much as I would love to savor this reunion and take shots at my wicked aunties, we have a problem."

The room was sweltering. Kayla was still in full-on flame mode. "What could be worse than *The Darkness*?"

Luke surprised Kayla with a blast of soothing energy. Now that he had a handle on his abilities, he knew how to use his power to shape emotion. Scarlett was happy to see him come into his own.

Beau's face said it all. Heartbreak and fear mingled with a fierce desire to protect. "Tia and Lilith are turning faster than we thought possible. They're preparing to murder Giovani."

Lava swirled in Scarlett's irises. The temperature in the room elevated and all metal within a one-foot radius was softening and glowing. "Lilith's blue fire isn't enough to overcome Father's. Who's helping them?" Everyone in the room took a careful step back.

Beau's expression was grim when he delivered the news. "Pyron..."

Scarlett's growl was primal. Rage swelled in her system, but she still knew their enemies didn't have enough power to kill Giovani.

"Jonah is the one they need to close the gap," Beau said with a straight face. This was no joke.

"How?" Scarlett was baffled.

Maxim answered for them with the creepy speaking-with-spirits voice. "He's the fire-wielding heir that Giovani has wanted all along. His mother was a fire witch and more...Jonah had no idea. She died before she could tell him. If she ever planned to tell him at all." Maxim trembled under the weight of his vision. Luke was at his side in moments, lending him strength. The contact was like a ripple in a still pond, cool and welcome. "His fire power had been dormant until the night that Magnolia was attacked. Pyron shared the truth of Jonah's lineage that morning."

Part of Scarlett was relieved that her judgment regarding Jonah's reliability and loyalty wasn't completely off. "He didn't seem strange until he 'showed up' after the attack and tossed me the pouch with the elixir." Scarlett bit her lower lip as something serious occurred to her. "Wait a minute, what could Jonah and Pyron get out of Magnolia taking the anti-aging potion? Why not poison her and be done with it?"

Beau took a long hard look at his niece. "They didn't want her to age. If she quickened, they would never be able to control her or access her powers."

"Is Jonah more powerful than Magnolia?" This

was the more pivotal issue. Scarlett hoped that they wouldn't be outclassed by the treacherous branch of the family tree.

Magnolia conjured *actual* lava and played with it as if it were cotton candy. "No Mama's sissy, Jonah doesn't haz more powers than me. I would have knowed it."

This was an interesting piece of information, which prompted her to ask another question. "Magnolia did you murder Rayne, or was it Jonah?"

The lava disappeared from the little girl's hands and sucked up all the excess fire magic wafting off Kayla and Scarlett. Scarlett was amused as she'd never been disarmed before. Magnolia's old soul owned up to her actions. "I blasted Rayne, and the fireball I sent through him ended up on Adriana's nightdress. Jonah was never there, just Rayne and my nanny."

"That actually makes some sense. Jonah was supposed to be there to protect her and must have been ordered to make himself scarce until the attack was over." Scarlett turned her attention to her best friend. Maxim had lost the dreamy expression and was now fully present in his own body. "Was Rayne supposed to fail?"

Maxim rubbed his chin in fake deep thought. "He was expendable. Jonah was not."

Jonah's confident demeanor when being questioned now made sense. For the first time in his life he was not alone, invisible, or powerless. "What could Auntie Evil and Uncle Flame offer Jonah that I could not?" Switching loyalties in one day was nearly impossible, especially with someone as steady as Jonah.

The air beside her wavered as Luke drew near. "Love, family, and a home. Some people would do anything to belong." Scarlett was proud of Luke. Sharing his secret with Tia had really turned his life around.

Kayla echoed that sentiment. "Finding home and family can change your life. I know it did for me."

"I could have given him those things." Scarlett was not defensive, just a bit clueless, a rare occurrence.

"You couldn't have given him Giovani's love and respect," Maxim countered.

Scarlett shook her head. "That's where he was wrong. Father is many things, but he wouldn't turn his back on Jonah once he knew the truth."

Beau took Scarlett's hand in his. "We know that, but Jonah doesn't. They took advantage of him."

"With the way Father has treated him, it wouldn't have been a hard sell," Scarlett confirmed.

Kayla picked up Magnolia and rocked her back and forth. "I wouldn't want Giovani's love if he treated me like crap. If he didn't love me for who I was before he knew of my powers, I wouldn't accept his love when he did."

Scarlett bit her lip as she weighed what Kayla said with what she knew about her father. "I get that, but power wouldn't be the thing that turned Giovani's head."

Magnolia rested against Kayla's shoulder, napping. "What would?" Kayla asked.

"Giovani has many children, more out of wedlock than in. Family is everything to him. If Jonah was his son, he would accept him with open arms."

Kayla wasn't convinced. "Rayne wasn't exactly feeling the love."

"Rayne's birth killed a woman Giovani loved. That's a hard obstacle to overcome. Later it was his character, not his powers, that turned Father off."

Magnolia picked up her head. Her eyes were sleepy, but her voice was strong, "Enough jibber jabber. We need to rescue Mama and Lilith."

Scarlett added her father to the list, along with Jet and Onyx. The room was crowded with too many questions and doubts, so she didn't bring up her cousins. There was one thing for sure: the boys would cast their lot with Giovani. Jet and Onyx had as much respect for their own father as Giovani had for Rayne.

"I agree with the little one. It's time to play hide and seek," Beau confirmed.

Chapter Thirty-eight

Cane waved her hand as she talked, which seemed normal enough until Lilith felt this odd peeling sensation, as if she was leaving the surface of her body, clothes and all, behind. When she gazed downward, she was still dressed. Lilith stopped and turned to look behind her. There was a version of the four of them, stopped in the clearing and talking to each other. "What the fuck, Cane?"

"We've had a busy little bee following us around for the past three hours, and it was time to lose her." Black smoke flowed from Cane's wrists, they looked like her black cobweb skirt. It was a wicked version of Spiderman. Lilith tracked the smoke as it grew and surrounded them. "I've pushed the illusion into the hunter's mind. She will waste her time tracking the false versions of us." Lilith didn't resist the magic as it closed in on her. The ground beneath them disappeared into nothingness. Tia screamed. A quick glance in her direction confirmed that she was freaked out by the transition rather than hurt.

The journey was cottony yet exhilarating. She loved the way Cane's magic felt—darkness spiced with evil. Lilith had never felt this way about the magic in Tia's house. Her own gifts always felt out of place, even though Kayla's flames were as deadly as her own blue fire. For a time, she liked being the darker one in the house, but fucking with people's minds and scaring the shit out of her classmates was getting old. The second Cane and her wife materialized, she felt like a puzzle piece clicking into place. They were Lilith's people. She was going along with the plan to kill Giovani because she loved the idea of ending the creep that had fucked up her life. If she was honest with herself, the idea of murdering someone was appealing. She was curious as to what would happen if she let her dark powers out full force.

The wasteland that they arrived in was a dark Goth fairytale. The black trees were leafless and the place reeked of violence and death. The sinister surroundings drew her in and a feeling of home spread through her system. Tia may be fighting her darkness, but Lilith was ready to revel. She had one question to ask before cutting her ties to White Magic Land. "Cane, did you have a hand in Angel's murder?"

Cane's aura didn't even flicker in response. She was eerily calm. "I loathe Belladonna. She has a nasty habit of seducing the young, even in spirit form. I'm glad that she will forever waste away in a state of constant pain and torment."

Morals, interesting. She figured being dark was an anything goes kind of situation. "No interest in minors?"

Cane's cackle had a dark burr to it, her laugher affected the air around her. Lilith was fascinated by a witch with no firepower that could make the air scorch. "Seducing teenagers is for the weak, it's like shooting a bird in a cage. Pitiful, no true challenge involved."

Lilith was surprised at the lack of resentment Cane's comment elicited. She wasn't talking down to her, merely stating facts. "Did she shoot a bird that you wish she hadn't?"

"Scarlett was fifteen." A flock of crows cawed and flew away from Cane's dark fury.

Silvia hissed. "The pale one is deliciously dark. Her virtue meant nothing to me. What I do care about is straight women fucking lesbians for entertainment. As if infidelity only applies to sex with men." Her hair was alive with tiny serpents that shared her disdain. Cane caressed her face. The snaky strands kissed Cane's fingertips. Reptilian love.

"Wicked," Lilith complimented. The lovers smiled in her direction. Tia was too quiet. She kept her distance. That was too bad, Tia would have to straighten her own shit out, fighting something that felt so good was a waste of time. Lilith wouldn't mind ditching Tia.

Cane spoke into Lilith's mind. *And we will, as soon as my brother sees Tia's murderous desire, she's expendable. Her role is to devastate Giovani.*

I thought they didn't see eye to eye. Why would he care? Lilith asked. Tia was willing to fight the demon blood coursing through her veins. It wasn't exactly a stretch to kill the man responsible for the dark polluting her light.

Giovani has a soft spot for all his children, but more importantly, Tia is Sophia's child. He loved Sophia like none other, before or since. The sap even tried to repress his own darkness for her. He failed of course, and she left him. Tia is a product of that love. Turning against him and seeking his death would maim his heart permanently.

The terrain was rough and getting steeper. When they turned around the bend, Tia gasped.

"Father."

Lilith could feel Tia falter. Demon blood or not,

she didn't have the heart for murder. Not when face-to-face with her father.

Cane had thought of that. The poison that leapt from Tia's lips was not her own. "You seem a little bit hung up. Shall I come back another time?" Cane was speaking through Tia. Lilith was surprised that Giovani didn't pick up on the ruse. "Though this will make it far easier for me to rip your heart out. That is if you still have one."

Chapter Thirty-nine

"That's not a very nice thing to say, Mama." Magnolia's voice was a blend of young and old, an emotional crossroad.

Scarlett didn't have words for what was in front of her at the moment. Her father was bound to a tree, had been badly beaten, and was crying silent tears. Those tears were Tia's tears—she did this. Even if Tia didn't mean to. Her intentions were irrelevant.

"Stop being mean to my No-no. He loves you and you are hurting his heart."

Tia gasped. The sound of her daughter's voice was strong enough to break the hold Cane obviously was imposing on Tia's mind. That was pure "mother's love" magic. It was far too strong for her bitch of an aunt to withstand. "Magnolia," was all Tia managed to say. She turned with the intention of running to her daughter's side. Cane dug her fingers into Tia's shoulder, making her scream. It wasn't the sharpness of her aunt's claws that made her sister cry out, it was the poisoned tips.

Cane's hands caught fire and she howled in pain. The flesh from her hands burned away completely, leaving only charred bones behind. Silvia tried to go to her lover but she found herself surrounded by a combination of snarling animals, some real, some supernatural. Luke had called every living animal in the Deadlands; there were more present than Scarlett thought possible. She heard howling in the distance, more beasts were on their way.

Pandora, not to be outdone, had called countless dead. She had much more to work with, considering how many people had met their end here. Pandora spoke to the ghosts. "Keep them here. No one gets in or out." The answering moans and raspy cries made the hair stand up on Scarlett's arms. The kid was a badass.

Now that her enemies were on notice, Scarlett went to free her father. Lilith's greeting was shocking. The bitch tried to fry her brain. "You may have caught me by surprise, Bluebelle, but you are *so* out of your league."

"Fuck you Bird Shit. I've had enough. You think you are so high and mighty." Lilith's distraction was giving Cane and Silvia hope, which made Scarlett smile.

The air around Scarlett rippled with heat as she called her strength and her dark power. She reached out her hand and clenched her fist, the action mirrored by a phantasm that cinched the teen's waist tightly. She raised Lilith until she was a good sixty feet in the air. "How high and mighty are you feeling now, Lilith?" Scarlett asked with saccharine sweetness.

Kayla was soon at Scarlett's side. She was horrified but didn't challenge Scarlett. Kayla whispered, "You're not going to hurt her, are you?"

I don't have to, Scarlett spoke into Kayla's mind. *I'm just giving Jet and Onyx time to scout the area and find where Pyron and Jonah are hiding.*

Kayla nodded. "I'll keep my eyes open."

Lilith looked down at them. "Kayla," she whimpered. The pain was only emotional. Scarlett was holding her up like a doll stand. She didn't need to crush her, to crush her.

Kayla's eyes were hard. "Are you so fickle that you can give up on all the people you love, to get vengeance on someone who has done you no harm?"

"No harm?" Lilith's voice was shrill.

Scarlett put a finger in her ear, pretending to soothe it.

"He ruined our first kiss by stealing Magnolia and brought this pasty white bitch into our lives. He's the reason Angel is dead. I lost everything," Lilith screamed. "I lost you," she added more quietly.

Jet and Onyx were in place, and her father's army was not far behind. The utility of distraction gone, she returned Lilith to the ground. She was even gentle.

Kayla was angry, but not heartless. She was at Lilith's side in no time, but for now she had nothing to say. Scarlett let the teens figure their own shit out. She had more important things to do.

Silvia was trying out her own beast mastery, but reptiles were wary of the ghosts and growing number of predators that were creeping into the Darklands. Once again, she was impressed by Luke's ability to call. There were more howls miles away in the mountains. It might take time, but she was glad the beastly reinforcements were on their way as well. "Luke," she called.

Luke's eyes were alive with pleasure, his magic was working beyond his wildest imagination. "Yeah?"

"I'm impressed."

Luke blushed.

Scarlett sensed Pyron and Jonah's presence. They had been there all along. Jonah was a far more skilled illusionist than she had ever given him credit for. He had to be. But now that she found the thread, it was easily tugged loose. "Jonah, I see you've come up in the world," Scarlet said with a trace of irony.

Jonah's aura shimmered. "You can see me?"

"Abso-fucking-lutely." Scarlett was moving imperceptibly closer. The motion was so slight, her uncle and Jonah didn't sense her advance. She had some mesmerism skills of her own. "I'm quite impressed. How did you manage to pin Father to the tree?"

Jonah's eyes were dark, with a flicker of fire licking up the black as if his eyes were coal briquettes catching flame. "Magic."

Scarlett rolled her eyes. "Seriously? Who was stupid enough to give you your powers back?"

Pyron's eyes glowed with anger. "Watch your mouth."

Jonah cast a wall of fire, keeping Pyron and Father within the circle. "Come no closer. Giovani will die more painfully if you intervene."

"Don't you mean 'Daddy'?"

The flames rose higher. Many of the animals and a few ghosts recoiled.

Magnolia, Kayla, and Lilith? Each name was an invitation. It was up to Lilith to grab the preserver or seal her fate with her new friends.

Cane called to her new recruit. "Lilith, Scarlett underestimates her new *brother*. He's the heir Giovani was longing for. Too bad he prefers to think of Pyron as his daddy. No accounting for taste." She shrugged. Cane's hands had healed themselves, but there would be scars. Should her auntie live through this event, each time she touches her beloved, she will see the scars and remember who gave them to her.

Lilith was torn between evil acceptance and hope. Kayla's dark expression wasn't helping matters. The choice was hers. There would be no welcoming party. She was in or permanently out.

Magnolia gripped Scarlett's left hand and took up Kayla's right. "Come Lilith, I loves you."

Sparks flowed and flickered around Lilith as she struggled.

Then Angel appeared. "Lilith, choose light. We are your true family."

Jonah's resentment made the circle of flame rise higher. "They will never respect you, Lilith. You will always be on the outside looking in, believe me. I know how that feels. We would never treat you the way they have."

"He's right," Angel confirmed. "They will never love you like we do."

Lilith was wavering.

"Come on, Sissy Blue Flames, join your real family," Angel taunted. She was grinning ear-to-ear when Lilith growled at her.

"Lies, you belong with us. Feel your magic and know your true place," Cane urged.

Scarlett smirked, knowing her auntie had said the wrong thing.

Lilith stalked toward Cane. Auntie's satisfied grin quickly turned into a scowl when the punk rock girl strode past her.

Scarlett was a little shocked that Lilith decided to grab her hand rather than Kayla's. Tia was the one to grab Kayla's hand. There was a ripple of power through the line as Tia amplified their firepower. The next surge of strength was all Kayla, and the Deadlands were engulfed in light. The intensity of which reflected the wild magic Kayla had been wielding in the house.

Magnolia, their leader, spoke next. "Jonah, you not plays nice with fiwer or your words. I take your fiwer now." She guided Kayla's hand so it connected with Scarlett's. Young Magnolia raised her chubby little hands in the air and called the flames from the ring of fire into her own body. She shone so brightly, Scarlett had to squint.

Jonah wasn't sure what to do. "Dad?" Pyron was horrified and promptly let his new son down. He fled but didn't get far.

"Uh-uh-uh. You're not going anywhere," Jet's words were quiet. He didn't need to raise his voice. Everyone heard him. Onyx blocked Jonah's route to escape. The executioners had truly arrived. At least that's what Pyron and Jonah thought.

"Jonah and Pyron, you have been very bad. I take your powers now," Magnolia declared sadly. "You hurt my No-no. I loves him."

Tia flinched but stood her ground. It wasn't just emotions that gave Tia pain; the poison Cane punctured through her skin had to be agony.

Magnolia put her hands out as if she was reaching for some cookies. "Powers come here, this instant."

Scarlett chortled. She could barely stand it.

Pyron and Jonah froze, their mouths open wider than could be comfortable. Their powers left their bodies and emerged as glowing spheres with fire licking at the transparent surface from the inside.

Vivian, her timing impeccable as always, called the orbs into a velvet-lined box. The lid snapped shut, the report was as sharp and violent as a shotgun blast. "Cane, darling, really." She shook her head, making her gorgeous ebony hair shimmer blue in the moonlight. "Did you really think you could fool me into following clones?"

"Don't lie, I saw your face," Cane countered. "You followed them."

Scarlett taunted her auntie. "Did *she* follow the clones or was it a false image of her own?"

"Daughter, I must say, you truly have livened up the place. I've had more fun in these months than I have in centuries. Shall I kill the Twisted Trysters?" Vivian's smile glowed, her incisors glimmered as if ready to sink into flesh. "Their souls are a bit musty, but I've tasted worse."

"Bitch," Silvia hissed, her forked serpent tongue fluttered.

"They's using bad words, I take their words." Magnolia called Cane and Silvia's voices first, then relieved them of their powers. The magic within Cane's sphere was a murky black and Silvia's was a smarmy green.

Vivian captured the four orbs in a green box. "The color of jealousy…fitting, is it not? Onyx darling, come fetch these boxes. They're *so* heavy." She pretended they weighed a ton, yet when they touched Onyx's hand, the objects were lighter than feathers. "Tut-tut, Giovani dear, what have I told you about bondage?"

Giovani's voice was rough from pain and lingering heartache. "I'll never learn."

Vivian floated until she could remove the bonds, and drew Giovani from the tree. Her burden was far heavier than the one she passed off to Onyx, but she bore the weight tenderly. Vivian cooed soothing words as she kissed his bruised brow.

"Daddy, I'm so sorry." This was the real Tia, who ached for her father. "Will you let me heal you? I'll be gentle."

Giovani forced his sleepy eyes open. "Of course, sweetheart. I trust you."

Tears coursed down Tia's face. "Daddy, I love

you. I'm so sorry I didn't trust you."

Scarlett stopped Tia from advancing. "You need to be healed yourself." She nodded at the angry claw marks on Tia's shoulders.

"Oh," Tia said in shock.

Luke appeared at Tia's side and tenderly healed the wounds. The poison oozed out of the gouges and soon the skin was pristine. "Now you can heal your father."

Tia smiled up at Luke. "I'm proud of you. You've grown into a fine young man."

Luke blushed, then professed, "I couldn't have done it without you, Mom."

Tia knelt by her father's side so her hands could hover over his many wounds. Tears ran down her cheeks as she sent healing energy into her father and helped to mend his skin.

Giovani looked weary, but he tried to smile as he spoke to his daughter. "I should have talked with you before I took Magnolia into my care. I only wanted to secure her safety."

She cupped his face and kissed his cheek. "Thank you, Daddy."

Magnolia, the mini fireball, ran up to Giovani and gave him kisses and cuddles. "I saves you right back, No-no."

"That you did, little one. That you did."

Epilogue

Lilith was silent on the trip back to the castle. Not that anyone was going out of their way to talk to her. That suited her fine, what could she say? *Sorry for being a traitor? I didn't mean to ditch you for the evil bitches.* Lilith had absolutely no idea what to do with herself. She couldn't go back to Tia's home after what she'd done, and there wasn't a safe place for her here in the Dark Realm.

The group was walking along the rose garden. Lilith spotted the bench where Magnolia and Giovani sat when they first met. She plucked a pink blossom and inhaled the sweet velvety fragrance.

"No-no has pretty flowers, that pink one is my favorite," Magnolia said. Her voice startled Lilith and made her drop the flower. "Here, I caught it. You hold it. Flowers make you feel better, 'kay?"

Lilith nodded. A mountain of roses couldn't erase the shame and sadness that weighed down her spirit. Magnolia tugged at her hand and tried to get her to join them in the castle for brunch.

"I'll catch up with you later," Lilith promised.

Magnolia climbed onto the bench, so she could look into Lilith's eyes. "I loves you." She cupped Lilith's face with her chubby little hands then laid a loud smacking kiss on Lilith's cheek.

It took effort, but Lilith was able to hold back her tears. "I love you, too, munchkin. See you in a bit. I want to enjoy the sunshine."

Magnolia gave her a hug, then hopped off the bench. "See you later, alligator."

"In a while, crocodile." Lilith sat on the bench and closed her eyes. She didn't want to see the looks of pity that they were bound to throw her way. Once the air quieted and the last steps faded, she opened her eyes. She gasped. Kayla was standing in front of her. Her expression held no pity, but the loathing she expected to find wasn't there either.

"Is there room enough for two?" Kayla asked.

There was something different about Lilith's first love. She didn't fidget or hide behind her long black bangs. Her blue eyes were bright and no longer haunted. Kayla was beautiful and confident. The battle had changed her for the better. That realization made Lilith's heart swell then contract painfully. She had never deserved Kayla's love in the first place. She would never be worthy of someone as strong and noble as Kayla.

"Well?" Kayla asked.

Lilith slid to the far edge of the bench, so Kayla wouldn't be forced to make contact with her body. "Sure."

Kayla sat in the middle of the bench. Their thighs touched. It was all Lilith could do not to gasp. The sensation was intense. Arousal blossomed in her stomach. She tried to talk her hormones down, but when Kayla took her hand and kissed her fingers, she failed. Her heart beat faster.

"I'm sorry." Kayla's expression was earnest. Her eyes were warm and full of something Lilith didn't dare believe.

"You have nothing to apologize for. I was the one who betrayed…everyone."

Kayla drew Lilith's hand into her lap, resting it on her black denim-clad thigh. "I abandoned you long before that. I was scared and it was easier to love a new little sister than be strong enough to love you back."

Lilith sucked in a breath. Small tears leaked from her eyes. "You don't love me anymore?" She figured as much, but hearing it this way sliced through her heart. She closed her eyes against the pain. The sensation of soft lips pressed against her own shocked the air from her lungs. She turned her head away to pant. "Kayla."

"Lilith honey, look at me."

Lilith couldn't risk it, she couldn't face the possibilities: pity, anger, uncertainty, or disappointment.

Kayla cupped Lilith's cheeks. Her firm yet gentle touch would broker no rejection. "Please open your eyes. I have something important to say and I need to look into your eyes when I do."

She slowly opened them and gasped. One look said it all: strong, confident Kayla loved her. "Kayla." Apparently saying more than one word at a time was beyond her.

"Lilith, the first time you told me you loved me, I was on the brink of death."

Lilith shuddered. Watching Kayla kill herself one missed meal at a time nearly broke her. It was bad enough to lose Angel, the only true friend she had ever known. She wouldn't have survived the loss of her first and only love.

"I never got to thank you for what you did, scaring me out of my funk." Kayla smirked then continued. "You told me you fuckin' loved me and kissed my socks off."

Lilith's laugh was as shaky as her emotions.

"The moment was stolen from us, and up until

recently, you were right to think Giovani stole it and ruined what was supposed to be a beautiful relationship."

"He ruined everything—" Lilith said with feeling.

Kayla kissed her lips, silencing whatever Lilith was about to say. This kiss was slow and methodical. Lilith was fully present this time around and she enjoyed every spine-tingling sensation. She moaned when Kayla deepened the kiss. The love and certainty behind Kayla's passion made Lilith feel alive...and happy. She stopped thinking altogether and allowed herself to feel, to be loved. For the first time in her life, she felt whole.

The sound of Magnolia giggling in the distance startled them apart. They panted while they caught their breath. Through the haze of pleasure, Lilith realized the sound didn't come from within the garden, it was wafting out of the window two stories up.

The next sound she heard gave her the giggles. It was Kayla's stomach. "The alien awakens."

Kayla smirked. "We better join them or I might be tempted to eat you."

Lilith's eyes widened when Kayla winked.

"One step at a time. For now, let's go join our family." Kayla helped an unsteady Lilith into a standing position. "After we eat our fill, I'm going to have a stern talk with Magnolia for interrupting our kisses."

"You wouldn't." Lilith was scandalized. She really liked this version of Kayla.

"No, I wouldn't. That would only get her to start asking questions neither of us want to answer." Kayla guided them past the rose gardens, into the cool stone hallway and up the grand staircase. "With our luck she would make a game of catching us in the act."

The little fireball ran full speed in their direction.

Scarlett caught Magnolia around the waist, then lifted her up. "Magnolia, our friends aren't bowling pins." She rested the toddler on her hip. In that moment, Scarlett actually looked eighteen. It was easy to forget Lilith and Scarlett were close in age.

"I wasn't going to bowl them. I was going to love them and hug them," Magnolia insisted.

Scarlett winked at the girls. "There will be plenty of time for that. First we need to feed Kayla's scary tummy before she starts gnawing Lilith's arm off."

Magnolia's eyes went round. Lilith smiled. There may be an old soul within the toddler, but she was a young girl at the same time. Lilith walked up and tweaked Magnolia's nose. "Now I got your nose, and if you want it back, you have to let us through. I'm not as starving as Kayla, but your nose might help me get rid of my hungries."

Magnolia squealed, squiggled out of Scarlett's arms, and ran full tilt as she shouted, "No-no, Lilith has my nose and she said she's going to eat it. Please No-no, get it back for me. I need my nose!"

Giovani's chuckle was deep and hearty. He walked up to Lilith and put out his hand. "May I have my granddaughter's nose back?"

Lilith rolled her eyes. "Oh, okay. You party pooper."

Magnolia chanted *party pooper* all the way down the hall into the dining room. She explained her near scrape to her mother, making Tia laugh. Tia picked Magnolia up and twirled her in a circle. Lilith smiled. This was the Tia she knew: loving, happy, and carefree.

Kayla shimmied past Scarlett and Lilith on her way to the buffet table. The two plates she filled would have sated a bus full of lumberjacks. Lilith had no idea where she put it all, since Kayla was skinny as a beanpole.

Scarlett leaned against the doorframe. "So, how you holdin' up?"

Lilith regarded Scarlett with curiosity rather than rancor. Her long white hair was down and rested around her shoulders like a veil. Her eyes were nearly white with a haze of violet. Scarlett's angular jaw and sharp features were at odds with her soft flowing hair and guileless smile. She was attractive in an androgynous way. "I'm better, but still kind of fucked up." Lilith was surprised with her own honesty.

"Understandable. This was a bit much, even for me." Scarlett sobered. "I lost my brother, my aunt and uncle, and was close to losing my entire family."

Lilith was a bit ashamed of herself. She was so wound up in her own drama that she failed to see what this turn of events would mean for Scarlett. "Your aunt isn't dead. What Magnolia did didn't kill her, did it?"

Scarlett's smile was grim. "She killed her in all the ways that matter. Without her powers or her voice, she is the living dead."

"Are you upset about that?"

"Nah, Cane brought this upon herself. She knew the score." Scarlett crossed her arms in front of her chest. "Her thirst for power was mangled by bitterness."

Lilith thought about those they left behind in the Deadlands. "Can they get their powers back?"

Scarlett shook her head. "Technically, that could be possible, if Father hadn't made their powerlessness permanent. Only someone of his blood could break the curse and return their powers, and they are fresh out of relatives willing to do so."

"Damn. So they're stuck there forever?"

"Pretty much." Scarlett didn't look sorry.

"What about those boxes, will they be lunch for Vivian?" Lilith wondered what her life would have been like if Vivian had been her mother. Being raised by a badass would have been a step up from her cruel, indifferent parents.

"Nah, she doesn't need their powers, and even Mother has her standards."

"How so?"

"They weren't her kills, and she'd rather eat glass than consume Cane and Silvia's twisted powers. Plus, she won't risk being stuck with their voices in her head for the rest of her life."

Lilith nodded. Kayla finished her first two plates and was going back for more. "Damn."

Scarlett clapped her hand on Lilith's shoulder. "Come on, let's join our family."

Lilith was rooted to the spot and her eyes reflected her state of shock. "Family?"

"Tia and her merry band of white magicians may not be your thing, but you fit right in with the demons in the family. So what do you say?" Scarlett gestured toward the long table filled with their chattering, robust family.

Lilith shucked off her pity party and decided to stop window shopping. "You're on." In no time she held her own towering plate of food.

Magnolia tapped the chair next to her. "Come on, Sissy Blue Flames. I saved you a seat."

Lilith giggled at the name Angel had given her. She rested her plate on the tablecloth and slid into the chair. For the first time in her life, Lilith had a seat at the table.

Liz & Shelia joint contact info:

Email: lizmcmullenandsheliapowell@gmail.com
Facebook: facebook.com/LizandShelia
Twitter: twitter.com/LizandShelia
Instagram: instagram.com/lizandshelia
Wattpad: wattpad.com/user/LizandShelia

About Shelia Powell

The first psychic-medium to be used on The Travel Channel's Ghost Adventures, Shelia is known for her special blend of homespun humor and gentle compassion. She has a large client base spanning several countries.

Shelia is a Certified Spiritual Coach, Intuitive, Empath, Medium, ULC Minister, and Reiki Master.

Shelia has been writing her whole life but finally published her first book, *Memoirs Of The Happy Lesbian Housewife*, which was a finalist for a Goldie Award under the nom de plume of Lorraine Howell. Her second book, written with Liz McMullen, *Finding Home* won the Goldie Award for Young Adult Fiction. She also has a book of poetry, *Becoming Me, A Metamorphosis*.

Shelia lives in Palm Beach County, FL. with her beloved Sweetie and their three dogs.

Contact Info:
Website: sheliapowell.com
Email: sheliapowellauthor@gmail.com
Facebook: facebook.com/sheliapowellauthor
Twitter:twitter.com/SheliaP_Psychic

About Liz McMullen

Liz McMullen has had a passion for history and world religions since she was a little girl looking up at her Dad as he told her stories. She fed her addiction to politics, history, mythology, and religion while at Mount Holyoke College and during her junior year abroad at Trinity College in Dublin, Ireland. She went backpacking around Europe, visiting all the places she had been reading about. Although her title as the Traveling Where's Waldo of the family has been retired, her wanderlust lives on in her writing.

Liz's debut novel, *If I Die Before I Wake,* is a Rainbow Award Finalist. Liz writes the *Finding Home* Series with her good friend Shelia Powell, who happens to be a gifted psychic medium. The series is set in Tia Keating's group home, where all of the foster kids have magical gifts. *Finding Home,* the first novel in this series, won a Goldie for Young Adult Fiction.

Contact info:
Website: lizmcmullen.wordpress.com
Email: lizmcmullenfiction@gmail.com
Facebook: www.facebook.com/Liz.McMullen.Author
Twitter: www.twitter.com/LizMcMullen

Other titles available by Shelia and Liz

Memoirs of the Happy Lesbian Housewife: You Can't Make This Stuff up Seriously! - ISBN - 978-1-939062-69-7

"A heartwarming reflection written with humor, wit and just the right amount of sarcasm, Lorraine Howell's fun and conversational style reels you in. Sit back and laugh as she shares what makes her "The Happy Lesbian Housewife." Jennie McNulty, Comedian, Co-host of LA Talk Radio show "Cathy is In, The Cathy DeBuono Show" and author of a weekly(ish) blog on Lesbian.com. With a partner named Sweetie, three grown children that are threatening to go into the witness protection program and a career as an adult entertainer, Lorraine Howell delivers a somber, no nonsense look at the difficulty of coming out late in life and how it has affected her poor, pitiful family...NOT! She really brings you a weight-loss book that guarantees that by simply reading her tome word for word, you will lose 25 pounds by the end. HA! Don't you wish? "Memoirs Of A Happy Lesbian Housewife - You Can't Make This Stuff Up. Seriously!" is truly a no-holds-barred, irreverent collection of stories looking at the late-blooming lesbian, Howell, and her hilarious take on life, love, friends, family and SEX! Nothing is off limits...Did we mention SEX? So hop on board and enjoy the ride. You will laugh and cry then laugh some more. Lorraine Howell's The Happy Lesbian Housewife, will not disappoint!

Becoming Me - A Metamorphosis - ISBN - 978-1-943353-51-4

"Becoming Me - A Metamorphosis" is a journey though the darkness and light of the human condition. It opens up discussions on deep and serious subject matters. It also

speaks of the joy and love that we all seek. "Becoming Me, A Metamorphosis" is an in-depth, raw, gritty and complex look into the human psyche. It is a beautiful journey of healing. This collection of poems sways your heart into the world of reality while keeping your emotions on edge. The purpose of this book is to deliver a profound and meaningful message to you, the reader.
Possible triggers

If I Die Before I Wake – ISBN - 978-1-943353-05-7

Charlie Dempsey has recently lost her beloved grandmother and is surprised to inherit a treasured family heirloom, the necklace her great grandmother wore on the boat from Ireland to the New World. But with possession of the necklace comes unwelcome and unseen guests that spark a paranormal awakening within Charlie and shakes up her once comfortable life as a first grade teacher in seaside college town. A dark spirit is stalking her, a ghostly child is haunting her, and she finds herself romantically drawn to Faith Lorian, a witch who is the key to unlocking the mystery of banishing the dark spirit once and for all. Together, can Charlie and Faith succeed, or will Charlie be irrevocably drawn into the darkness determined to ensnare her?

Unspoken - ISBN – 978-1-943353-35-4

Desiree Chevalier is determined to control her own destiny, and that includes shaking her mother's iron grip on her life. Rosalie Chevalier is not going down without a fight. She's a corporate raider after all and it just wouldn't do to have a wayward daughter. When Desiree steps away from the Chevalier fortune to put herself through Mount

Holyoke College, Rosalie decides to show up on her doorstep. Although her mother digs in, Desiree refuses to bend.

Rowan Knight is working just as hard as Desiree to put herself through school. She is intrigued by Desiree but also wary of the icy reception she receives each time they meet. Rosalie's persistent interference in Desiree's life intensifies the tension between Desiree and Rowan. Will they be able to move past the obstacles in their path, or will their love remain unspoken?

Finding Home - ISBN - 978-1-943353-04-0

Firestarter Kayla Cruise has been kicked out of another foster home, her twelfth, and she's back at the railroad tracks where she always finds solace. Surprisingly, a woman shows up there as an apparition, offering something Kayla had been longing for all her life, a forever home. Not just any home, Tia Keating runs a group home for teens with special gifts…gifts like the ones Kayla has spent years running from.

The problem is that when something feels like it is too good to be true, it usually is. Evil is stalking Kayla and her new family. The Darkness is putting her dream placement in jeopardy. It also threatens a burgeoning relationship that Kayla doesn't quite understand, as well as the only true family she has ever known.

With the help of Tia and the rest of the family, Kayla is going to fight back. The demons won't get to take away her happiness, not this time. Will this placement be her Lucky Thirteen or will The Darkness destroy Kayla's hope for a happily ever after?